THE UNREMARKABLE

ENTRIES IN THE JOURNAL OF GORDON GRAY

THE UNREMARKABLE

T.A. GALLANT

TIMOTHEOS PRESS

The Unremarkable: entries in the journal of Gordon Gray

Published by Timotheos Press
Nashville, TN

Timotheos Press is an imprint of Pactum Reformanda Publishing.

Body text typeset in Garamond Premier Pro.

ISBN-13: 978-0-9972447-1-7

For all the ordinary people,
whose power is love.

ENTRIES

IN THE JOURNAL

OF GORDON GRAY

After all that has happened, I suppose it's appropriate to start with the basics. My name is Gordon Gray.

That's right. Not something interesting like Brumby or Dunstable, or even Johnson.

Just Gray. Gordon Gray.

Every Gordon I have ever met has been ugly. Not the sort of extraordinary ugliness you might meet in the interesting characters of film noir — the bulbous nose, the crooked mouth, the squinty eye, the monumental brow, the exaggerated jawline, something memorable and distinctive. Something to latch on to, something to pull us in.

We can't look away from train wrecks. Protest as we may, we are not at all repulsed by the extraordinary, even if it is profoundly unattractive. "Characters" engage our attention.

Gordons do not engage our attention. We look past them without so much as being aware we are doing so. Gordons are forgettably ugly in the most English and interminably dull sort of ways. Gordons are ugly only in a way that a Gordon would bother to comment upon.

Take me, for instance, if you must. My nose is just a bit too thin and a bit too long, but it needs to be pointed out — sorry, I couldn't help myself, which is another of my prosaic traits — for you really to notice.

My lips are slightly thinner than average, and quite nearly angle inward, so I carry around a perpetual but subtle pinched expression.

I have a narrow chin, and it sits just a bit too far back to be manly.

My hair is coarse but thin, straight, and medium brown, and essentially unstyleable.

They say that brown eyes are the most beautiful.

Not necessarily.

My eyes are brown, but naturally not the brilliant sort of brown that fascinates the artist. My eyes, like me, could aptly be described as dull and forgettable.

My dear old Dad dropped me quite on my face when I was barely more than a baby. My Mum assures me that it didn't harm my looks.

In other words, the damage had already been done.

I dress conventionally, adorned only by a dreary gray fedora.

I am the ordinary, the unremarkable, in person.

To be sure, everyone, no matter how unremarkably ugly, is said to have the opportunity to have a beautiful, exciting life — an engaging career, a fascinating hobby, quirky skills, unexpected gifts.

Not Gordons, and certainly not me.

My parents emigrated to America when I was nine. Not to someplace glamorous like New York, but to Midfield, a dull town just outside of Arburo, the most bland city of the American midwest.

Or so I have heard; I am not a tourist, and have not seen the places most people seem to find alluring.

From my name, you may deduce that we ourselves were not interesting immigrants, landing upon these shores from some exotic locale. Nor were we dissidents fleeing repression in the midst of the Cold War. If you will indulge me for a moment — we arrived from England a few years after the war, not due to a sense of adventure but because Father's firm had been procured by American business interests, and the bombings had destroyed our neighborhood. So at the company's invitation, we arrived in the midwest, virtually by default.

You are now informed regarding the most mildly interesting thing about me — my foreign past. My upbringing resulted in a lingering but rather indistinct Kentish accent (so Mum says), and of course I never learned to say "apartment" rather than "flat," and so on.

I have not sought to alter the trajectory set by my heritage and early monotonies. To the contrary, I have settled quite comfortably and contently into ongoing midlife monotonies.

I work for Mr Clark Green, CPA, as an office administrator. In other words, my calling entails doing the things that even an accountant finds too boring to trifle with.

Mr Green's offices are on the second floor of a nondescript building too far out of the downtown core to be trendy, and too close to downtown to be upscale. The only thing unconventional about our working habitat is that in a world of overweening familiarity, Mr Green insists that we address each other by our surnames, which suits the remnants of my English sensibilities.

I would assert that I have extracurricular pasttimes, but concede that I am rather unrelenting in my dullness. I was told by my therapist that having a hobby would be healthy, but most hobbies are quite expensive, and I was raised to be frugal. My parents were old enough to have survived the Depression, and learned never to waste a thing. Mum still has half a room full of old egg cartons, and when he passed, Father left the garage full of empty oil cans. We shall not even begin to speak of used fasteners and containers of every variation known to modern man.

Well, out of a sense of duty, I started collecting. I collect various fragrances of hand soap. It's not that I am fastidious about cleanliness — at least, no more so than other Gordons, although that is unlikely to be an unimpeachable point of reference. I suspect that as a group we are a bit more averse to dirt than, say, Toms. Mark Twain could not have named his character "Gordon Sawyer," of that you may be sure.

The thing about soap is that I can readily obtain most brands for a quarter or so, and less with coupons. Moreover, the bars are small; the new hobby required no significant effort in arranging space for the collection.

About the therapist — don't get the wrong idea. I lack the requisite emotional or intellectual life to require the sort of therapist you likely have in mind. My therapist, Robert, is actually a physical therapist who helped me out a couple years ago when my hand failed to heal properly after I cut myself on a broken mirror.

The cut hand was the biggest adventure I experienced in my twenties, but did not involve violence toward the mirror, just to be clear. Apparently, the mirror was lacking the proper clips; the backing tape supporting it gave way while I was standing in front of the sink, and the glass shattered on my bony hand as I was vainly and foolishly attempting to break its fall.

Occasional coffees (or rather, tea, in my case) with Robert continued after the completion of treatment, and that is how the collecting came about. He is an avid railroad modeler himself, and he urged me to cultivate a pasttime.

I do read rather voraciously and play chess given opportunity. Furthermore, I enjoy feeding pigeons at the park, accompanied by my pipe. But apparently those activities are of no account in Robert's particular ordering of hobbyist values, and as he is, by default, my apparent hobby guru, it became clear that I had to broaden my horizons.

So soap collection it is.

The periodic meetings with Robert have been the extent of my social life for quite some time. As you see, I do not get out much.

To be sure, it was not always this way. After college (I earned a nondescript two year degree in office procedures), everyone thought it necessary to "network," and for a while I got invited to various parties and events. But it seems I have an overly keen eye for detail, a fixation with precision, and the sort of humor that is too strained, too self-conscious, to strike the correct party mood. At the last party to which I was invited, I managed to ask what most crucial element was missing from Mendeleev's periodic table, and got no response. No response, either, when I delivered the punchline, "Surprise." The guests around me pretended not to be talking to me at all, and drifted away with their eyes fixed on their drinks.

I live simply. My modest flat lacks even a tiny balcony; my "yard" consists of a bracket which I have contrived to attach to my bedroom windowsill.

Upon this bracket, I have affixed a small bird feeder. As with my other ventures, this effort's reward has been meager; as a rule, the creatures of the air studiously ignore it. The sole exception is a solitary Carolina chickadee that visits me nearly every evening. I have come to love that bird.

As you may have gathered, my one extraordinary characteristic is in fact an extension of my utter ordinariness. I notice virtually everything, and can recall altogether too much of it. I have a nearly limitless capacity for tolerating minute details. Mr Green appreciates it, but in retrospect, it was the death of my short-lived party-going. Hearing yourself described as pedantic, boring, and insufferable (along with some undesirable traits, as well), and knowing it's all true, confirms that you have no future as a social butterfly.

I am Gordon Gray, and my life has been as colorless as my name.

Uneventful, and unremarkable.

At least, until I met Astoria.

Today was odd, which does not happen to me. Nothing is ever odd, which is how I like it.

I didn't see it coming. How could I? Nothing unusual ever occurs, so I can scarcely anticipate it.

Everything started like every other weekday of my life: opening the office around 7:40 a.m. and sorting the mail, Mr Green arriving at 8 a.m. sharp, working until noon, taking a modest half hour brown bag lunch, returning to the office and working some more, and finally departing at 3:30 p.m. I have been in the employ of Mr Green for nearly nine years, and these days vary little. I am a man of ritual, and I appreciate that.

So I blame the Industrial Revolution.

It was the bus.

I took route 43, as always. Route 37 is a bit more direct, but it has few public restrooms on the route. I don't mind the warehouses and rundown districts of 37 — they have to be put somewhere, after all. But sometimes, you need to follow the lead of your bladder.

Note to self: unnecessary detail.

It was the same bus arriving at the same time with the same smell of diesel fumes, the same driver wearing the same expression and wearing the same cap at the same unnatural angle.

All was right with the world.

I turned from paying my fare, the usual jangle of coins still ringing in my ears. At that very moment, that familiar world was lost to me forever. It was then I first saw her, sitting two rows in to my left, wearing a white blouse, a trim chocolate jacket, and a light brown cloche hat.

I am not above noticing a beautiful woman, and she was beautiful. Consequently, I noticed her. The sort of woman who can't quite blend in even if she's trying, which I rather think she *was*. Dark silky hair with just the slightest hint of auburn, rich red lips, eyes that were the *right* color of brown, and exuding the smoky sort of feminine softness that makes men's knees turn to hot butter.

I walked by, and I swear I felt her power. Certainly, my knees did.

Even crazier, I sensed her attention. I cannot explain why, but I felt those entrancing eyes following me all the way to where I came to stop upon entry, a hand loop near the back. There were no more empty seats, but the standing room was not too crowded, at least, and remarkably, no one was smoking. Certainly, I have had worse luck on 43 this year.

I had barely settled in when she joined me. Although she appeared to have endeavored rather unsuccessfully to dress for the secretarial pool, there was something extraordinary about her. Something that told me she was strong and confident; that she didn't belong here, and yet that she could belong very nearly anywhere if she chose.

At any rate, she didn't look the type who often stood on a bus — or rode one at all.

Meanwhile, I didn't look the type who often was approached by a beautiful woman on the bus, or anywhere else.

She opened brightly, "Rather full today, isn't it?"

"Yes, it is. I'm rather surprised you sacrificed your seat."

"Oh, I *did* need a stretch. These seats are insufferable after a few blocks." I couldn't argue with that. So I didn't.

Glancing at my ringless left hand clutching to the loop, she extended her right. "You can call me Astoria," she smiled, but informed me in a confidential tone that the name is assumed. Her real name is "too exotic," and she's looking to find a life more ordinary; and anyway, I surely wouldn't be able to pronounce her real name.

On that score, she was surely wrong: I have excellent phonetic skills and a keen ear, but I restrained myself from correcting her.

The fact that I was standing on the bus talking to a beautiful woman who had sought me out may seem fantastic to you — as it was to me. (The only less likely scenario would be me finding the courage to seek *her* out.)

But it happened. I'm still weighing *why* it happened, but it happened.

"So, you take this bus often?"

"Every weekday. It's the best route to my place of work."

"What do you do?"

I told her, reluctantly — not because I am ashamed of my profession, but because I was idly wondering whether she were in fact some sort of criminal. But if she already knew where I worked, she need not have asked, and in any case, I could see no advantage she could gain from knowledge of my employment.

So I told her, and her eyes glittered as if what she had heard were too good to be true, a grand stroke of luck. "How very lovely," she exclaimed without the slightest hint of insincerity.

"I don't know about that," I replied, "but it's quite nearly a living, since I have simple tastes."

"Tell me more about your job."

I looked at her dubiously. No one, male nor female, had ever requested further information upon hearing the nature of my career, although me being me, I had not necessarily restrained myself from offering it.

"I mostly provide organization. I have spent a number of years perfecting a specialized filing system for Mr Green. Accountants are numbers-oriented, and I have developed a way to file things based on, shall we call it, *case severity,* rather than — say — alphabetical order. Mr Green likes to tell me, 'Pay attention to the dates. The dates are important.' Which, of course, they are. But I am always able to find the file he is looking for in less than two minutes.

"Besides being in charge of files, I am on hand to notate Mr Green's personal meetings with clients, although I must concede most of his conversations take place over the telephone, and he handles all calls himself."

She was enthralled.

I know what you are thinking. All of this is a mere tale. In real life, extraordinarily beautiful women do not walk up to unremarkably ugly men and start something. Such women do not approach strangers on buses. They live in a world which is hermetically sealed off from men such as myself. Men like me are more likely to engage in interplanetary travel than to be accosted by exotic females.

But you haven't met Astoria.

I had the same sort of assumptions, and so I was forthright. "May I ask you something?"

"Certainly."

"What possessed you to come talk to a stranger on a bus?"

"Sorry, what was your name?"

"Gordon. Gordon Gray."

"And what brand are you?"

"I'm sorry?"

"I mean are you a Catholic, a free-thinker, an Episcopalian, what?"

"Oh. Anglican."

"Okay, Gordon Gray, so you're not a stranger, are you? I know your name, I know where you work, what you do, what sort of faith you belong to, and what sort of man you are."

"Well, you didn't when you approached me. And I could be lying. And anyway, I should think that knowing those things wouldn't have provided much in the way of ... encouragement, you know."

She smiled enigmatically, which seemed suitable.

"Look, Gordon Gray, I gather that you think you are the dullest man alive. You have no idea what I would give for a dull life and a dull man. I have had adventures and escapades to last me several lifetimes. For me, I would embrace" — and with the word *embrace,* I really did think she was about to put her arms around me — "I would embrace the ordinary in a heartbeat."

I smiled too, but not enigmatically. Wanly, perhaps. "My dear, it would be quite strenuous for me to aspire to become ordinary. Even the ordinary is remarkable. I am not remarkable in the least."

Astoria's eyes laughed at me. "Gordon Gray, so candid! But please, don't devalue yourself. I can tell you're solid and stolid, and that's a sight better than the playboys who are full of self-regard and style themselves as fascinating."

"Do you always assess people so rapidly? Any stranger on this bus could be a serial killer, you know. Were you aware that Vincent Devens, who killed seventeen people over the course of four years, was also an office administrator for a CPA? Or that Richard Fearce rode the same bus every day for twelve years, and they still haven't ascertained the full count of victims he found on his route? I wouldn't think talking to strangers would be a reliable method to escape adventure and danger."

"Okay, then, Gordon Gray," she replied without missing a beat. "Are you a serial killer?"

"Not that I am aware of."

"Well, then, we shall get on splendidly. When is our stop?"

And so it seems to have begun, this strangest of friendships between an unremarkable man and the most remarkable woman I have ever met.

FIRST ENTRY

So Astoria stayed in my flat last night. I had not expected her to get off at my stop, as you may imagine. But then, I hadn't reason to expect her to approach me, or to have anything at all to do with me. So what's one more wonder among so many?

Were I more anxious, I suppose I may have been more concerned that *she* were the serial killer. I still cannot help but feel there must be some ulterior motive, but my imagination fails me at this point. What could such a motive possibly be? I am neither rich nor connected nor initiated into arcane mysteries; so far as I am aware, there is nothing to gain from knowing me.

And yet, that does seem to be the aim. It became clear last evening that she wanted to know all about Gordon Gray — a new experience for me.

For my part, *I* tried to learn more about *her,* but if she didn't exactly come across as evasive, neither was she enthusiastically forthcoming. Always, Astoria was very committed to bringing the topic of discussion back to me. Most men find this flattering. I frankly find it a bit unnerving. Other than in my journal, I do not prefer to talk about myself.

I did learn that (according to her own term) her brand is Presbyterian; that she is a secretary downtown; that she lives halfway across the city; and that she was on the 43 because she had missed her own bus.

The only personal thing she told me was that her mother had passed away some time ago; but when questioned, she was apparently uneager to provide further details. I could gather that her mother's loss remains a sore spot.

So, over soup and tea, and on into the evening, we talked about me: how I grew up, what my family was like, what my Dad had done before his passing, what my Mum does, what interests me, where I have been. Gripping fare, to be sure.

After an evening of what I assumed was dull conversation for her, Astoria made her way toward the bedroom. I grabbed a couple of blankets and a couple meager pillows from the linen closet and arranged them on the sofa. Astoria stood in the bedroom doorway and looked at me. "Surely you're not going to sleep there?"

"Quite naturally. You are my guest."

She cocked her head slightly. Clearly, she knew I was feigning ignorance of what she meant. "You're a good man, Gordon Gray," she said softly.

"My Mum will be gratified to hear it," I rejoined, although I was quite sure Mum wouldn't be too approving of a woman spending the night in my flat. "Have a good sleep, Miss Astoria." I thought of my little piece of the outdoors in my bedroom, and hoped she would enjoy the music of the Carolina chickadee.

I heard the door close, and hauled my legs up, resting my feet on the far arm of the couch. As I pulled the blankets over myself, I wondered vaguely if the bed would in fact be as much too firm for Astoria as the couch was too soft for me.

And then, I slept.

SECOND ENTRY

I awakened early this morning with my senses full to a world of wonder. I was acutely aware of the smell of breakfast cooking and coffee brewing, the spitting of the frying pan, and the vibes of the Beach Boys.

Half sitting up, I looked across to the little kitchen. "Good morning. Lovely choice in music."

Astoria turned, looking startled.

And comical. She had borrowed my headphones and plugged them into my compact kitchen radio. The bulky equipment on her head made her look like an alien from one of those science fiction movies of the decade just past. A beautiful alien.

She glanced at the radio connection and looked back at me. "You surely can't hear that?" By way of answer, I started to sing along, but as always I was flat, so I stopped. I squinted at the volume dial, although (as I discovered in doing so) squinting was unnecessary. It was set at two.

Her eyes followed mine. "You have good ears," she said.

"But not a good ear," I quipped. I was rather proud of that one. "The bacon and eggs are making me hungry. And the grits, too." Even as I said it, I was taken aback by the notion. I should not be able to smell something as very nearly odorless as grits over the aroma of bacon and coffee, or really anything else.

"Grits?" She looked at me quizzically. "I think I've heard of them, but I've surely never had them, and I am definitely not *making* them. I can try, if you tell me what I would need." She glanced doubtfully toward the cupboards.

"Oh? but I smell them…." Even as I spoke, however, it occurred to me that I had no cornmeal in the flat. Astoria could scarcely have made grits even had she intended to.

Odd.

I frowned, put on my slippers, and leaned out the front door into the hallway. Astoria trailed me, bemused. I could still smell the grits. Raising my eyebrows at her, I followed the smell until I got to number 439 at the far end of the hall. "Ah," I said, and looked at Astoria. "Do you smell that?"

"Well, maybe, but…." She looked back down the hallway, and so did I.

It was absurd; I could see that much. The door to my flat was some sixty yards back.

Dishonesty really is not in my nature, but I recovered quickly and forced a laugh. "I got you good there, didn't I? Billy Joe is from Georgia. He makes grits every morning right about now."

She gave me a faint smile. "Okay, Gordon Gray. Yes, you had me there." She paused a second. "Maybe you are a *little* bit odder than I thought." We sauntered back to the flat and had breakfast.

The coffee was surprisingly good. Being English-ish, I typically breakfast with tea, but there it was in my cupboard along with the French press (a gift from Mr Green years ago), so Astoria had prepared it.

The rest of the repast was suitable, although it was plain that the woman is not well-practiced in the culinary arts. I quietly surmised that she had not grown up helping in the kitchen and that her hand at the stove had come quite recently. But I am a simple man, and gratitude is a valuable commodity.

"Well, Mr Gray," she said, as the time neared for me to depart for my workday, "this really will not do, you know. You get to call me something mysterious like Astoria. I cannot very well be calling you Gordon."

"Well, it is my name, after all."

"True enough, but Astoria isn't *mine,* which isn't fair play. Hmm." Astoria sighed. "Not to worry, I shall think of something." She pecked me slyly on the cheek. "Don't be late for work."

Never. That would be unpredictable, and as a rule I am averse to unpredictable.

Astoria, however, is unpredictable. I am willing to make an exception for Astoria, just this once, to see where it goes.

THIRD ENTRY

When I got off the 43 to walk the final three blocks to work, I headed toward the pretzel vendor who posts just around the corner on 83rd. I couldn't smell the pretzels until I was within forty yards — about the same distance from which I had always smelled them.

I had not heard anything more than usual on the bus ride, either.

I glanced toward the news vendor. I had to squint to read the headline of *The Weekly Gossip*. "Trendy Local Socialite Dies in High Speed Crash." I walked closer until I could read the subtitle. "Blake Quarters Dead at 29." I tilted my head and gauged my distance. My eyesight was apparently normal.

Now, at least.

I shrugged, and headed for the office. Clearly, my senses are no more acute than they ever have been. Had I imagined about the grits? But what then of the Beach Boys?

Never mind. I glanced at the Carolina chickadee perched on the first floor windowsill, and took the stairs up to Mr Green's offices.

Mr Clark Green is a small, overly-serious man who walks with small, overly-serious strides and grimaces when he smiles. He is quiet even when speaking emphatically, but he has two loud children, and one even louder wife. She is garrulous and gushing, using friendly words in a way that makes you feel quite assaulted. Her name, reputedly, is Helen, but Mr Green, staid as he is, calls her Mrs Clamor, and occasionally (when extremely irritated) Helen Brimstone.

Never, however, within her earshot.

Mrs Clamor comes by the office every so often to harangue her husband about something or other. I try my best not to eavesdrop, but that is rather like electing to not hear a passing train while standing next to the tracks. The matters of conversation generally tend to be things which would be better left unsaid, or could easily have been addressed at home, but she prefers to bring them to Mr Green's office.

I tell myself it is because she dearly loves him, and wants to see him more. The intrinsic unlikelihood of the sentiment does not deter me. I can be stubborn in my optimism when it suits me.

Mrs Helen Green chose today to drop by and attempt to provoke her husband. Perhaps it is sport for her; it is very nearly impossible to get a rise out of Mr Green, and anyway, she gets her way with invariable certainty. His capitulation to her whims is somewhere parallel to death and taxes.

Apparently, the visit was necessary. She had come to announce that they needed new living room furniture, posthaste, and he must buy the set of her choosing no later than tonight. Mr Green sat quietly at his chair, bearing her tirade and stroking his chin in a manner that suggested to himself that he was carefully considering her proposal, when in reality all three of us knew that Mr Green would do precisely as she wished without argument. But he does his best to convince himself that he makes domestic decisions.

I dutifully rustled my papers and cleared my throat, trying to avoid over-hearing the elongated description of the hideous fabric pattern Mrs Green had picked out for her new furniture. Apparently a faux leather in garish orange with yellow and lime green inlays. A delight to the eye, to be sure.

As I filed today's new folders, my mind wandered back to Astoria. I tried to picture her as a Mrs Clamor, but the experiment failed. From my obser-vations so far, Astoria's personality is sufficiently strong that she need not resort to domineering obnoxiousness, and she is able to care about someone's interests other than her own.

I wondered if I would see her again, or if the preceding day had been a blip, a glitch in the system that would never recur. Everything about the pre-vious evening and this morning suggested the former, but the utter unlikeli-hood of it all inclined me to tell myself that I had seen the last of her, and my life would revert to the same unremarkable routines.

I wasn't sure whether to be comforted or frightened by that thought.

That's when I knew that she had already changed me forever. There is no going back.

> How sweet are Thy words to my taste! yea, sweeter than honey
> to my mouth! Through Thy precepts I get understanding:
> therefore I hate every false way.

So the adventure continues. When I emerged from the office yesterday afternoon, Astoria was awaiting me on a nearby bench. Had I provided her the address of my office the previous evening? We had talked extensively about my work, so it seemed possible. But I couldn't remember, and I'm usually pretty solid about details.

Perhaps infatuation is clouding my capabilities. I'm sure that's never happened to me before, but I've never met Astoria before.

It was sunny, in the mid-eighties, and she had folded her jacket upon her lap. She was reading something called *The Edible Woman,* but looked rather weary of it, even though she did not appear to be all that far in. When she saw me, she rolled her eyes slightly, stood up, and flipped the book into the bin beside her.

Bemused, I asked, "What was that about?"

"Oh, more drivel about how awful the ordinary is. I'll return to reading *Slaughterhouse-Five.* After yesterday, perhaps that's more appropriate, anyway. How was your day?"

"Ordinary," I grinned. "Utterly ordinary."

"Excellent. You and I shall get along fine!" We strolled toward the bus stop, she grabbing my arm with both hands and leaning her head against my shoulder.

And just like that, there it all was again. The transfiguration of my senses. Everything about me seemed to come alive, and I was acutely aware of it all. I could hear dogs and mice, shopkeepers and doorbells. I could smell perfumes and colognes, body odors and exhausts. I could see the individual pores of Astoria's skin, I could discern each singular speck of color in her brown eyes. I glanced across the street, and discovered that I could read the smallest of lettering on the smallest of signs in the shop windows. I overheard the low tones of a conversation between two businessmen nearly half a block away, sufficiently to gather the gist of the discussion.

My chest tightened, but I forced myself to be cheery, and it had to be Astoria herself, unaware of my perplexity, who helped me feel at ease. She spoke of foreign wars and Vonnegut and of human suffering, and unintentionally, reminded me that the world's problems are much bigger than my own, and in the middle of it all, sprinkled in a few melodic lines of "Let It Be," and I learned to enjoy the emerging layers of this strange woman.

While we waited at the bus stop, I warned her that the sixties hadn't made a hippie out of me, for one, and there would be no further sleepovers. I would put her in a taxi to return to her own apartment at the end of the evening.

She didn't look either offended or relieved, but somehow I got the sense that, after all, she thoroughly approved of an old school gentleman. I haven't decided yet whether she is an old school lady who has got a little bit lost, or a modern woman who, for whatever reason, is *trying* to. Perhaps it is a bit of both.

She is slowly opening up bit by bit. Over dinner (I made potato soup), I learned that she is essentially estranged from her father. After her mother's death, he gradually became increasingly obsessive with his business. "He was always absorbed, from the time I was tiny. I was his only child, but I never seemed to get much time with him, at least, not time where he wasn't working.

"Then after Mama passed, it got worse, much worse. He started to block everything out. Even when he wasn't just ignoring me, he always seemed to be calculating. Yes, even with me, figuring how to gain advantage from his assumption that I was beautiful."

Astoria used the word *beautiful* matter-of-factly, with neither vanity nor false modesty. This was something altogether new to me. I have met other women who also had justified confidence in their appearance, but they had a haughtiness — a sort of princess mentality — that Astoria does not seem to share. It's like she realizes that her aesthetic riches, as it were, do not make her better than anyone else.

She went on, "Really, he tried to use me as a pawn —" and she stopped when she saw the look on my face.

"No, not quite like that. I mean, he hired me as a corporate rep — a 'company ambassador,' he called me — which largely means he took me along to meet business prospects, especially if they were single. It's like he was sort of dangling me in front of them to distract them. Anything for an advantage. I even dated a couple of them a handful of times, although I have to admit that he never suggested anything like that. But all the same, I started to feel like it was all wrong, that there was some kind of invisible pressure, however unintended, and began to feel dirty about it all. About the business, about my father, about everything.

"Already before that, we were growing apart. I think it grated on me most that he never wanted to talk about Mama, and in my youth, I felt like he was deliberately forgetting her, and it hurt. I blamed him. I felt like he hadn't really loved her, that she didn't matter to him. I wanted to talk about her, remember her. I wanted to share that with him, to honor who she was. And he couldn't, or wouldn't.

"And then, too, it seemed he was always angry with me, which was partly my fault, I suppose. I had to get away from him, so I would go on trips — often enough, trips officially made for the company — and I spent a bit too much of his money in Europe. I became fanatical about Europe; he became fanatical about his money. It got to where we couldn't talk at all anymore. So my last trip, I stayed away a long time, and when I came back stateside, I didn't even tell him. I just left everything at home and started over."

I really was trying to focus upon this estrangement between Astoria and her father, and I was also eager to encourage her to remember her mother, to help her get all of that out, because clearly, she needs to. Still, when she mentioned Europe, I couldn't help but think for just a moment:

Oh, dear. She's a spender.

It was a passing thought at most, but apparently something showed on my face. Astoria is remarkably intuitive about some things, at least, and seemed to read my mind. She gave me a sideways smile. "I know what you're thinking! I know you said you were economical. Believe it or not, so am I. I tried the high-flying life long enough. Since I've returned, I've managed to live pretty comfortably on a secretary's wage without once touching my old account." She looked at me and smiled. "You don't think I can keep it up, do you?"

"I don't know. People do change, although I don't really believe that I for one have changed all that much." I shrugged a little, and said slowly, "I guess I'd be worried that you're viewing frugality as some sort of penance. That, I think, would get old rather quickly."

Astoria looked thoughtful. "No, it's not penance," she said at last. "This is really me. I mean, I like nice things, but I have always been ambivalent about extravagance. I was reckless with money, a bit, in Europe, but it wasn't *shopping*. Possessions have never been my bag, as they say. Most of the spending was travel related; it seemed I was always chasing one adventure after another with whomever I was with. I think I can very safely say I'm done with that."

I studied her, trying to ascertain whether she was trying to reassure *me,* or *herself.*

She smiled at me. "Well, at any rate, we have spent two evenings together, and we have eaten simply and entertained ourselves modestly." I looked at her, wondering if this were a reproach. But clearly it was not. "Gordon, my point is that I have been completely comfortable with that. It's exactly what I want."

After she left, I admitted to myself that I had no clue what was happening.

Get wisdom, and whatever else you get, get insight.

FIRST ENTRY

Last night, Astoria asked me if I had ever stayed at the Waldorf Astoria. I told her I rarely have seen the inside of a hotel at all, much less the Waldorf, since I really don't travel, and that seems rather a concomitant circumstance. It's true that I went back to the UK to attend my Aunt Elizabeth's funeral two years ago, but I rather think that doesn't count, and anyway, I stayed at my cousin's house.

Then too, we're talking about *me,* and even were I a traveller, I'm far too economical to be taking up at anything resembling the Waldorf.

So, needless to say, now Astoria has taken to calling me Waldorf. Clearly thinks she's being clever, and I suppose she is.

I don't mind, really, even if she's being ironic. With a name like mine, who could complain? I haven't asked whether Waldorf replaces Gordon or Gray, but so be it. It can replace both, if it's coming from her lips.

Astoria is a genuine enigma. She is at once surprisingly frank and highly private. While she has invested herself heavily in learning about me, it has been more difficult for me to pry open her own shell. I tried on Thursday to get her to talk about her mother. After all, her father's silence on the subject had contributed to their estrangement; that fact, and the longing in her voice, made clear that she is hungry for that sort of conversation.

But she can't do it with me, not yet.

I'm slowly learning about her, though. This morning, for instance, I took the direct route. I'd asked the question before, but wanted to probe further.

"Okay, I really need to know: why did you strike up a conversation with me on that bus? I don't have — I think they call it, 'low self-esteem' — but at

23

the same time, I know what I am. I'm a very plain and dull fellow, and to be painfully honest, beautiful women do not generally track me down even if they know me."

She flashed a hint of that little crooked smile I'm growing to know and love. "Waldorf, you'd have to know a bit about my life. To be honest, I'm frightfully tired of being surrounded by remarkable, larger-than-life men. I hope you're not offended when I tell you that it was the very fact that you seemed utterly *un*remarkable that drew me to you."

"I am never offended by the truth," I said. "That is just the word for me. Unremarkable."

"Anyway, it started with my father. Everybody calls him a genius because he did some things years ago that people thought impossible. Then when I got older, I ended up with a string of boyfriends —" She stopped and looked at me apologetically, even regretfully.

I waved my hand. "I would scarcely have expected otherwise."

"Anyway, it seemed like each one of them had some crazy ability that made them ... *extraordinary*."

"Remarkable, huh?"

"Exactly. Like my last one. He drove like mad, which drove *me* crazy — but he could do *anything* behind a steering wheel. He drove in ways that defied the laws of physics. I mean, it seemed his driving skills were superhuman.

"I'll never forget for the rest of my life that day when I knew I just had to stop with these extraordinary men. We were careening through this winding mountain pass in the Alps at a ridiculous speed, starting a very long descent from near the peak.

"And all of a sudden, a wheel comes off, and there's this — I don't know — thousand foot drop right beside us, no guard railing, nothing. I really thought I was about to meet the spirit in the sky."

She stuck out her tongue and sighed. "Here we are, going probably a hundred miles an hour down this mountain, missing a wheel, the road is slippery, the car is practically sideways, and he just calmly shifts gears, steers and brakes like this magician, and we stop at the side of the road, perfectly safe. And what does the man do? He just looks at me, gives me a big grin, and shrugs."

Astoria shook her head at the memory. "It was too much, and this sort of thing keeps happening to me, I keep finding men like this. He was just ... the last in a series.

"So I swore then and there that even though I quite cared for him, it was all over for me. Not just with *him,* but with everything extraordinary, everything that smells of adventure. I just want ... I just want a normal life, Waldorf."

I smiled wryly. "I don't know if dull is normal, but I definitely do not smell of adventure, at any rate."

And even as I said it, I sensed that I was being somewhat dishonest toward myself. This relationship to Astoria, whatever it is, is uncomfortably adventurous. Not simply because romance itself is an adventure for a solitary soul such as I, but because I continue to find my senses gaining unnatural powers whenever we are together.

Even there, at that table, I could hear car doors closing down the street and all sorts of sounds of the city which I had never before been able to discern. I could see the individual colors in the tightly woven fabric of the sofa on the far side of my flat. I could hear the heartbeat of my companion, although she sat across the table from me.

I would have been afraid, except that there is something about her that makes me feel more powerful, more capable, than I have ever thought I really am.

SECOND ENTRY

This morning, I called my Mum. She reminded me that it had been three weeks since I had been at Midfield, and asked if I would be coming out.

25

"Soon, Mum. But, uh … my life has got a little more *complicated* this week."

"How's that, Gordon?"

"I've met someone, Mum, and honestly, I don't really know what to think."

"Oh, Gordon, that's wonderful! You know I have been praying for you to find someone. What's she like?" She stopped short. "She's *baptized,* isn't she, Gordon?"

"Yes. That is, I think so. I would suppose, since she's Presbyterian. They baptize infants, don't they? The thing is that she seems very private, which is the one thing that concerns me, Mum. I don't know how easy it is going to be to get to know her."

"So, tell me all about it. How did you meet? What made you decide to get involved with her if she's so secretive?"

"It's a rather odd story," I said. "I can scarcely believe how it happened myself." And so I recounted the meeting on the bus and the evening that followed, carefully omitting any mention of Astoria staying over.

"Well, that is rather … *unusual,*" Mum observed, with no small emphasis. "But what do you like about her if she is so, ah, restrained, about herself?"

"Well … I should probably tell you that she is extraordinarily beautiful," I admitted.

"Well, good. Charm is deceitful, and beauty is vain."

"I know, Mum, I know," I laughed. "But there's a lot more than that. I suppose part of it is that she seems genuinely interested in *me,* for who I am. And she's warm, intelligent. And for whatever reason, we seem to really … *connect,* something to which I am unaccustomed. I'm just taking things slowly, wondering, really. I really like her, but I don't know where this is going quite yet."

"Mmhmm. Does she come from a good family, Gordon? You don't actually know, do you?"

It was difficult to answer that.

"All I really know is that her mother died young, and her father got all wrapped up in his work. He's some sort of businessman."

"So, she doesn't have a good relationship with her father? That's often a warning sign, Gordon."

I could scarcely argue with that. "That's true, Mum. Good fathering is an important part of the shaping of character. But she seems to have pretty good character nonetheless. So far as I can tell at this point, the rift really seems to be because he worships mammon, and she does not. And also how he seems to have tried to forget about his wife after she passed. A child needs those memories, needs healing, and he didn't give that to her. But I know there's always the other side of the story. I'll try to reserve judgment until I have opportunity to get to know him."

"That's good, Gordon. Take it slow. And bring her to see me! I'm quite a good judge of character myself, you know."

I smiled at the telephone.

"I know you are, Mum. And I'll do my best to get her out to see you."

My soul doth magnify the Lord, and my spirit hath rejoiced in God my Savior. For He hath regarded the low estate of His handmaiden: for, behold, from henceforth all generations shall call me blessed. For He that is mighty hath done to me great things; and holy is His name.

I have to admit that I was rather curious how the weekend would go. It's one thing for two people to entertain one another for a couple hours of an evening; it is rather another to throw them together for a day.

Throw into the mix that one of them is the dullest man alive, and the recipe may not go quite as one could wish.

As it turned out, I need not have worried.

Saturday, Astoria arrived with very definite plans. We were to go to a driving range, and then to early lunch. I gravely told her I was an avid golfer; that I had once shot a 62. The second hole, however, was considerably worse.

She bears with my humor bravely. In turn, I endured the driving range. In truth, it was quite fun, even if not the activity I would have thought to choose, and I was quite embarrassingly bad, as my athletic aptitude lands somewhere between chess and backgammon. Whatever heightened capabilities have overtaken my five senses, the hopelessness of my sense of coordination persists.

On the bright side, my floundering efforts gave me the occasion to see Astoria giggle, which I don't think I had previously witnessed. And it was rather sweet that on a couple occasions she stood behind me, grabbed me by the elbows and shoulders, and attempted to improve my swinging posture. The effort was vain, of course, but we both enjoyed the comedy.

She, of course, was brilliant, her drive fluid and graceful, just as I knew it would be. She is surprisingly modest for such a remarkable woman, and declined to tell me what her handicap is, but even my inexpert eye assured me she is well-trained in the arts of golf, confirming what has become pretty clear: this is no ordinary working-class girl. I suppose that is unsurprising, given what little she has told me about her background. Working-class girls do not travel Europe on company expense accounts.

We dined afterward at a modest establishment suitable for a couple earning office wages. The food, however was fine, although "very unimaginatively" (Astoria said) I chose fish and chips, which is my quasi-English go-to if I am unsure whether to trust the menu. For the sake of marine comradeship, Astoria elected for a seafood salad, whose diminutive portion compelled her to pilfer just a few of my chips.

I've heard that such pilfering of chips is a tradition among couples, so I suppose we are now a couple.

We spent the afternoon reading to one another in my flat, me from P. G. Wodehouse (she seemed really happy of that appreciation), her from Graham Greene, and closed the day together with the improbable combination of chicken salad sandwiches and goblets of merlot. Astoria claimed the choice was exquisite. She doesn't fool me, but I nonetheless appreciate her harmless fib.

The second half of the weekend was as wonderful as the first. Come Sunday, she was already at the door at 7:30 a.m., adorned with a pretty floral sundress and a straw hat, and equipped with a blanket and a basket crammed with all manner of things requisite for a kingly picnic.

After breakfast, however, the radio weatherman informed us that the patterns had shifted, and we could expect a steady rain until mid-afternoon.

Astoria proved herself undeterred; she spread the blanket on the floor, and coolly unpacked the basket of all its wondrous goods. It was not time to eat, and so she made the absurd proposal of a walk in the rain, with which naturally I complied. Above her objections — she really did seem to think it quite jolly to get a little wet — I brought my trusty umbrella and shielded us from the drops of heaven, she clutching my arm and commenting gaily on the mundane scenery of the neighborhood.

We walked a wide circuit of a couple miles in this fashion, adopting a leisurely, conversational pace, and making our reappearance at my building shortly past 10:30.

I pulled her inside and grinned at her. The umbrella services notwith-standing, Astoria was glistening with rain. I thought it time for a quote out of context.

> *You gave me hyacinths first a year ago;*
> *'They called me the hyacinth girl.'*
> *— Yet when we came back, late, from the Hyacinth garden,*
> *Your arms full, and your hair wet, I could not*
> *Speak....*

She didn't miss a beat:

> *And if it rains, a closed car at four.*
> *And we shall play a game of chess,*
> *Pressing lidless eyes and waiting for a knock upon the door.*

And then, when we got back inside the flat, she proceeded to the picnic basket and pulled out a volume of T. S. Eliot. In response, I pulled out my set of chess. And we both laughed.

I think I like this girl.

Astoria is a thinker, too. I'm afraid she wrestles with issues more than I often do. I get a sense that her circle of knowledge and interest is rather larger than mine. I think about the route to work; she thinks geopolitics. I mean, I suppose I do too, just not with her sophistication.

Just when I was going to use my knight to take her rook, she asked me what I thought of George Kahin. I remembered reading something about him regarding Viet Nam, but could not offer much of an opinion other than questioning whether he had Communist sympathies.

She promptly declared checkmate, and we both laughed again.

I then introduced her to *Dies Natalis,* and we both cried.

There's something about being able to share the emotional gamut with someone ... outside of Mum, I don't think I've experienced this before.

Since I made it clear last Thursday that I was not becoming a flower child, Astoria has been the portrait of conscientiousness, invariably saying her goodnights before 9 pm.

Last night, however, Finzi, the poetry and the merlot had their effect, and she seemed to lose track of time.

So I did what I always do around 9:15; I pulled out my prayer book and knelt down with it open on a dining chair.

In my peripheral vision, I saw her tilt her head. "What are you doing?"

"The daily office."

"What's *that?*"

"Evening prayers."

"Oh, of course. It's been so long ... Father was Presbyterian, but he stopped going to church after Mama passed. She was always the praying one, really, anyway." She got a hint of a faraway look in her eyes.

"Well, if you want to distance yourself from your father, this would be an excellent way to be unlike him," I smiled gently.

Astoria laughed. "I like it. Prayer as an act of rebellion."

"It always has been," I said, as she knelt at the chair beside me.

"We didn't use a book," she noted, glancing at mine.

> *Worship the Lord in the beauty of holiness; let the whole earth tremble before him. O God, make speed to save us. O Lord, make haste to help us.*

When we finished, Astoria was quiet a moment. "That passage about building bigger barns — he really meant that, didn't he? I knew someone a lot like that." The flat grew quiet, and the sound of the ticking of the clock filled my ears.

"Yes," I said. "We all can find ways to store up all sorts of treasures which we make important to ourselves, and yet be in utter poverty regarding things that really matter."

"Well," she said, "I rather like your prayer book. I feel I don't pray much because I don't really feel like I know how. Having some words to help me along seems like a good idea."

"I try to do both, but the prayers in the daily office remind me that I am praying along with others — many others, millions. There's something reassuring about that to me." I looked back at the bookcase beside my sofa. "Say, I have an old copy of the Book of Common Prayer. Why don't you have it?" I got up, plucked it off the shelf, and handed it to her.

Astoria opened the flyleaf and looked at me. "Oh, Waldorf — I can't take this!"

She held the open book in front of me, and I glanced down.

> *Dear Gordon,*
> *Congratulations on your confirmation. No matter what happens, we will always be praying with you and for you.*
> *Love, Dad and Mum*

My confirmation. Back when Dad was young and healthy, and we wrestled in the living room, and Mum chided us good-naturedly.

I sheepishly admitted that I had quite forgotten the source of my "old" prayer book. I took it from her hands and replaced it with the newer one from which we had just read.

"Thank you," she smiled, gave me a goodnight peck on the cheek, and took her leave.

I touched my cheek for a moment, and headed for bed.

The strangeness is getting stranger still.

Up until today, everything surreal occurred only when I was with Astoria. I had been testing it almost daily, and felt certain that the newfound powers of my senses were directly attributable to her presence. Which, of course, I could not explain in the slightest, but somehow found to be of some consolation. Whatever it all might mean, that left things all on her side, and there was no hint that I myself was somehow changing.

This morning, however, the pattern bled out into my non-Astoria life, and it was rather unnerving. From my flat, I could distinctly make out the song of my lone Carolina chickadee half a block away. I could comprehend muttered conversations several rows behind me on the bus. Before I even made my exit onto the sidewalk, I could smell the vendor's pretzels. I could read the subtitle of *The Weekly Gossip* without breaking stride.

By the time I reached the door of Mr Green's offices, I was nearly shaking. What sort of witchcraft could this be? I unlocked the door, tossed my jacket onto the coatrack, and collapsed into one of the leather waiting-chairs. It was 7:39 a.m.

My mind was abuzz. Does this mean, after all, that Astoria is *not* the source of all this? or does it mean, rather, that somehow, her power over me is growing? How? Am I unconsciously feeding it, in some indeterminate and unintended manner?

For that matter, is she aware of any of this?

On that point, I was fairly certain of a negative answer. I recalled how earnestly she had spoken to me of her anxiousness to get away from extraordinary men. To this point, she had been, if not oblivious to my newfound powers, at least not acutely aware of them. If I could trace everything to some odd power she had, she herself at any rate seemed unaware of it.

But, assuming this was about *her,* why was the power changing, growing? And what did it mean?

I could not answer, and still cannot.

Seeking to becalm myself, I repeated the daily office for the second time that morning, then picked up the mail which I had neglected on the floor, organized it, and laid it sorted on Mr Green's desk. I retreated to my own, and proceeded to engage myself in what he had left out for me the previous evening. I completed my tasks, and glanced up at the clock, wondering where my employer could possibly be.

That couldn't be right. 7:51 a.m. That's only twelve minutes since I arrived. It takes that long just to get through the daily office. I pulled out my pocket watch and stared in confusion. 7:51 a.m. Had I been dreaming? I glanced back to my desk. Everything was done.

A long while later, at 7:55 a.m., Mr Green entered. He looked at me, then at my desk, then again at me. "You did that already? What time did you get here?"

"I arrived early," I admitted. No earlier than usual, but he need not know that.

"Mr Gray, you know I value your conscientiousness, but I am getting a bit concerned. I think your work is starting to consume you. You need to get some sleep. And for God's sake, *please* find yourself a good woman!"

Oh, the irony.

He glanced around. "No newspaper?"

"Hasn't arrived. You're not wanting it already, are you, Mr Green?"

He looked at me steadily. "I guess you haven't heard yet."

"About what, sir?"

"There's a bloody civil war over in Kent at the university."

"What, over Viet Nam again?"

"Yes, they're protesting the launch into Cambodia. The National Guard
—"

I was lost. "Cambodia?"

"Mr Gray, do you even read the news? The President announced last
Thursday that he had authorized a campaign into Cambodia."

*After yesterday. She said that Friday…. So that's what Astoria meant when
she was talking about Slaughter-House Five.* My heightened senses notwithstanding, I was in the dark. I hadn't been looking at the papers (since
Wednesday, naturally), and Astoria and I had better things to do than listen
to the radio news. She was being rather more specific than I had realized
when she was expostulating upon foreign wars and human suffering yesterday.

I feel like such a lunkhead.

My employer looked at me seriously. "Mr Gray, I don't think you are well."

Mr Green sent me home at lunch, quite certain that I had been at the
office at least since four. I'm sure I looked sufficiently haggard to support that
notion, but that look was not due to sleeplessness. It was because I was frightened of what was happening to me.

I lunched on the sidewalk bench, then walked back home instead of riding
the bus, arriving at 12:27 p.m. Which is utterly impossible, but so be it.

So here I am. I have already cleaned my flat twice and read three books
this afternoon.

I wish I had called Astoria, or could have. Now she is probably waiting
for me outside the office, or at my bus stop. But still, she has not let me in far
enough to give me her number.

This secretiveness makes me uneasy.

SECOND   ENTRY

Shortly past five, the telephone rang. "Waldorf? Oh, I'm so glad you're
home!" She sounded horrible. Was she crying?

"I'm so sorry I didn't wait around for you. Mr Green gave me the afternoon off, and I don't ... I was unable to call you."

"Oh, don't trouble yourself about that," she responded rather faintly. "I became very ill over the course of the night, and haven't been out of my room."

"Oh, I'm so sorry. Can I come over? I could bring you some chicken soup or something."

She declined, but this time I heard the reluctance in her voice. I don't know what is tearing her in two, but I find it hard to bear.

"Waldorf, this morning I had the weirdest dreams — no, I'm not even sure they were dreams, it was probably delirium. I don't know. Whatever it was, I was stuck in this timeless state, feeling wretched, and the worst part was, in my dream or vision, time stopped. It was like I was sick, eternally heaving and retching. Oh, Waldorf, sorry to be so graphic, but it was awful."

"Astoria —"

"Waldorf, do you suppose that's what hell is like?"

"Hell?" I thought a moment. "Well," I said slowly, "feeling miserable and afflicted and being alone, with no sense of the passage of time because it goes on and on without ending. Yes, I suppose that would be a rather suitable description of hell."

Silence a moment. "Waldorf?"

"Yes?"

"It's — hell isn't *real,* is it?"

"I certainly hope so."

She nearly gasped. "Why would you *hope* such a thing?"

"Because I hope for justice, and the present world quite clearly is inadequate in providing it. Do you think Hitler or Stalin got their just deserts?"

She sighed, and I thought this was a bit too much for a sick woman. I was very nearly about to apologize, or at least steer the conversation onto another track, but then she said, "That doesn't sound very *ordinary* of you, Waldorf."

"Well, I'm a rather *old* sort of ordinary, Astoria. I don't have the capability of being ordinary in this newfangled fashion. I don't really understand it."

"I think I'm changing my mind about you, you know."

"Oh?" I held my breath, dreading what she may say next.

"I actually think you are pretty remarkable in your own way."

"Thanks, I think," and I meant it. I didn't want her to think of me as exceptional. Our deepening bond seemed to me to be under threat by such a development. "Most people think I'm just pedantic, which isn't particularly remarkable."

"Well, your kind of ordinary is pretty extraordinary to me." She heaved. "Waldorf, I think I need to go back to bed. I miss you."

"I miss you, too. I hope someday you will — that is, I hope someday I can look after you when you are like this."

"I hope so, too. Goodnight, Waldorf."

"Goodnight."

I hope so, too. That's something to hold onto.

Tend the sick, Lord Christ; give rest to the weary, bless the dying, soothe the suffering, pity the afflicted, shield the joyous; and all for your love's sake. Amen.

The weirdness with time that occurred this past Monday has not recurred, thank God.

That is not to say that things have returned to normal. I think normal has ceased to exist. Or at least, the new normal is that my senses are far more powerful than makes logical sense. I would say that my senses have always been *keen,* but never anything like this.

I have definitely decided that Astoria is the source of these new ... powers. It *has* to be her.

It's true that as of this week, I still have extraordinary abilities even when I am *not* with her. That much is new.

But even now, when I *am* with her is generally when things *really* explode. Normally (ha!) it is the usual five senses that simply have become almost comically acute. I am also much more aware of multiple things at once.

With her, recently I have started ... *knowing* things without any access from my five senses. Or, it seems like it's knowledge. Some of these things, I have not verified, and don't know how to do so; it's just a powerful sense that I have.

Take this morning, for instance.

We were playing chess again, I was working up a variation on Alekhine's Gun, and we were cheerfully bantering about the merits of popular music and its sociological impact, perhaps prompted by hearing "American Woman" on my little radio.

And then a thought came to me out of the blue, completely unrelated to everything we had been hearing, doing, and saying.

"Astoria," I said suddenly, without any forethought: "you need to call your father."

Her smile faded. "Please don't ask me to do that," she said quietly.

"I think there's something wrong," I said, and then realized how that must sound. I was not being careful enough.

"Why would you think that?" I could almost swear that she had a worried look, and was ready to ask me something, but stopped herself.

"Well, I really don't know. Lately, I've been getting these odd feelings — intuitions. It's not like me at all."

I so wanted to tip my hand, even just a little. I wanted to say: *I think it's because I'm 'in tune' with you somehow. I can sense things through you before you are even aware of them yourself.*

But of course that's going to sound like bunk, or at the very least, turn me into something awfully remarkable, and where would that get me?

So I held my tongue, and my hand remained untipped.

"Oh, I get intuitions too — although not really about my father. I — I don't think about him."

I could see she was lying. Mostly to herself.

I said nothing.

I still cannot shake the feeling that something is wrong, that her father needs to see her for some reason. But my feeling is scarcely a compelling argument. I don't even know her father.

Now, the likelihood of my intuition being accurate would seem to me to be highly improbable. And so it *did* seem to me, this morning.

But then, midway through the afternoon, it happened again, albeit at rather a more trivial level. While we were discussing the relative merits or demerits of Dickens, something in my mind told me that Astoria was having a craving for Chinese food, and would want to go to the Red Bowl for supper.

We have never gone to the Red Bowl, and so far as I can recall, Astoria has never indicated an affinity for Chinese food.

But at four o-clock, she suddenly turned to me and said, "Waldorf, I am already getting a bit hungry. Have you ever been to the Red Bowl? I suddenly have a craving for some good Chinese cuisine."

I must have gone a little pale, because she asked, "What's wrong? Do you dislike Chinese? It's okay; we can eat somewhere else.... Or we can eat here, that would be better —"

"No, no, it's alright," I replied, recovering quickly. "I think I'm a little light-headed. Probably getting a little hungry myself. The Red Bowl sounds great."

And so she was none the wiser, but apparently, I am.

But why?

> *He has shown the strength of His arm, He has scattered the proud in their conceit. He has cast down the mighty from their thrones, and has lifted up the lowly. He has filled the hungry with good things, and the rich He has sent away empty.*

We finally got our picnic today. Astoria returned with her floral sundress, her straw hat, and her picnic basket, and this time the weather cooperated. The sun was radiant, the heavens were clear, and a quiet breeze crept across the surface of the city.

As I pulled out my tobacco paraphernalia, she exclaimed, "I didn't know you smoked a pipe!"

"Only on Saturdays, and only outdoors," I replied. "I needn't bring it if it bothers you. It's one of my rather antiquated customs, but not a particularly necessary one."

"Oh, no," she interrupted, "I quite like a pipe. It brings back happy memories."

"Your father?"

"Nah, he's a cigar man. My Granddad was the pipe man. He used to perch me on his knee and support me with one hand, and work his pipe with the other, and tell me stories."

"Multi-talented."

"Yes, very." She smiled and slapped me softly on the shoulder.

"Well," I said in a deliberative tone, "I don't know whether I can perch you on my knee...."

"I'm quite sure you could," she said, unsuccessfully trying to look offended. "I really don't weigh that much."

"I was going to say, I don't know whether I can perch you on my knee while smoking a pipe, but I'm pretty certain I can tell you stories. You see, I'm very limited in my multi-talented-ness."

"I have my doubts about that."

Down we walked to Livingston Park, enjoying the late spring bloom, and found a spot near my favorite bench to spread the blanket. In the back of my mind, I knew I was aware of all manner of things, such as the markings on the new jumbo jet leaving a trail above us, the sound of screeching brakes on the bus stopping a block or so over, and the smell of the cocker spaniel across the park.

But none of that bothers me anymore; I am accustomed to it, and have largely learned to master it, especially when I am with Astoria. I can scarcely believe that I already have become so comfortable with my own utter strangeness.

I do remain unnerved about one thing, however. I still am getting signals from somewhere that Astoria needs to contact her father, that something is wrong, and even a sense that time is running out.

Of course, given her earlier response, I have not brought the matter up again, and deep down near the pit of my stomach, I feel it, this ... edginess, quite like a sense of constant guilt, or the dread of an impending unpleasant and difficult task.

But these disturbances aside, days like these are too wonderful to allow to be spoiled. So, as I always do, I focused on its delights rather than my inner struggle. I was determined that we both enjoy ourselves, and we did.

As we settled in, a number of the pigeons and sparrows recognized me and approached expectantly, albeit at a cautious distance.

"You're quite a celebrity here, I see," Astoria observed with a small smile.

"My one arena of notoriety," I replied, as I flicked a bread crumb toward a particularly avaricious-looking bird. The pigeon struck out violently at the innocent crumb, which immediately succumbed, undoubtedly in mortal agony.

Astoria chuckled at the eagerness of the pigeon, and turned to me. "Well, my dear Waldorf, as has apparently become my custom, I have brought along a reading selection," waving her hand toward the picnic basket. "But ... I think you need to tell me a story instead."

"I'm game," said I. "Fact or fiction?"

"You choose, but don't tell me. Let me believe it could be truth *or* fantasy."

"Good fantasy is truth," I said, "if not particularly factual."

"I can out-pedant you, Gordon Gray, so watch your step!"

I looked at my feet and very nearly commented that I was not walking at the moment, but held my tongue. A glance told me she already knew the thought that had crossed my mind, and she just shook her head hopelessly, rolling her eyes just a little.

I involuntarily gave her what felt like a rather foolish grin, and commenced my tale.

"All right. Once upon a time, or, if you will, a definite and certain number of years ago, in early Spring during the lives of people you've likely heard of, there also lived a man of the Earth."

"Likely. Go on."

"This man of the Earth, for the sake of convenient reference, we will call ... Barry."

"Berry?"

"Yes, Barry."

"Okay, Berry."

"Barry was an inveterate humanoid, and refused to act the part of an animal, as all good people do."

"Shocking!"

"Indeed. Barry grew up, got a job, got married, had children, still worked that job, and eventually died, leaving them a modest inheritance."

"Could this really have happened?" Astoria queried.

"Well, these days, scarcely," I intimated. "But in Barry's day, it was within the realm of possibility, albeit both unusual and a point of widespread controversy."

"Surely. What did Berry work at?"

"Apparently he worked on a farm."

"Well, naturally. A berry farm, no doubt. But what exactly is a 'farm'? The term seems to be of recent coinage."

"Its apparent recency is only due to its archaic antiquity. According to the linguists, it fell out of common parlance precisely 463 years, two months, and sixteen days ago. At any rate, back to the word's determined meaning: It seems that in days of yore, people grew things out of the dirt."

"Like, automobiles and couches?"

"This may have been before automobiles. I don't know about couches."

"Before automobiles? Such a time seems inconceivable. Okay, so what then would one typically grow out of the dirt?"

"Various forms of plastics, I suppose. Keep in mind, the records are very obscure at this point. No one really knows much about those days, other than that Barry was employed on one of these 'farms.'"

"Fascinating. Is the story over?"

"It appears to be, as Barry is dead."

"That's so sad."

"Well, maybe not for Barry."

"What modest inheritance did he leave for his children?"

"An automobile and a couch, I think."

"I thought that this all happened before automobiles."

"Well, if this is a fantasy, anything is possible. If, on the other hand, it is fact, perhaps automobiles were invented late in Barry's lifetime. So you will have to choose whether you believe the truth of this story as fact, or as fantasy."

"I think it all happened just as you said, although I really don't think your hero's name really was Berry."

"What do you suppose it was?"

"I don't know." She glanced at me with a mischievous grin. "Gordon, maybe."

"Ah."

"Nah. That's too modern. How about Patrick?"

"Patrick? Astoria, that was my Dad's name!"

"What? No way! Maybe I'm remembering something subconsciously. Had you told me that? Or maybe his name is somewhere in your apartment?"

"Hm, I don't think so, but we've talked about him, so maybe I did tell you. Anyway, I'm telling you now: his name was Patrick!"

She clapped her hands at the serendipity, and prompted me for another story, even better than the first.

And so went our day. Even I, the dull Gordon Gray, am learning to bond through the high art of whimsy.

But I cannot forget her father, whoever he is.

> *Even the sparrow has found a home, and the swallow a nest*
> *for herself, where she may lay her young — even Thine altars,*
> *O LORD of hosts, my King and my God!*

It's over.

We quarrelled last night, and I think I very nearly went to jail. But that wasn't the worst of it.

It all began after dinner. We got off at the 134th Street stop, because Diedrich's Diner is one of my few favorite haunts, and we needed supper. To be perfectly candid, I have been a bit negligent with my shopping this week. I've been spending my time with Astoria, which is really no excuse, because we could have shopped together.

But none of that matters now.

Back to Diedrich's Diner.

I may be socially inept, but even I am well aware that Diedrich's is not really the place to treat a lady, and it's not the best part of the city, either. But I am an inveterate creature of habit, and as new and unexpected as the relationship with Astoria has been, other than the accidental discovery of the Red Bowl, I never did work up the will to discover a new place to dine.

Besides, Diedrich's provides a good sincerity test. If Astoria were really interested in my plain life and plain tastes, there is no better ordeal than navigating the drab atmosphere, humdrum service, and unassuming menu of Diedrich's.

The mood, however, was not the problem. Turns out the woman enjoys diner food, or at least does a reasonable facsimile of pretending to do so.

It's after we left the diner that everything came crashing down.

In many respects, I would be quite right to maintain that it was all Astoria's fault, really. But I should have known better. Rather than heading back to the bus stop, she pointed to the cross street running left off 134th. "What's down there?"

"Not much that I know of. I don't explore around here. I do know that in the first block, there's an old cluster of shops that was quite the hubbub during the war, but has been deteriorating for fifteen years of more. Most of the buildings are empty now. Beyond that, I really have no idea, but I'm sure it's not all that pleasant."

She can be impulsive. "I should like to see it."

I was hesitant. "Astoria, it's getting pretty dark, there's a fog settling in, and the bus is due in six minutes...."

"We can get the one after that. I never really get to see this side of things, you know. The fog will only make it more romantic. It shall be quite fun."

Romantic. She said, "romantic."

And so, we trundled onto Deadmarch Street, dusk falling. She was quiet for a couple blocks, and I started musing that at least we weren't riding a subway in Queens.

It happened just as I was turning to her to plead that it was time to head back. At that moment, in the rapidly deepening darkness, a man burst from the shadows, snatched the necklace from Astoria's neck, and disappeared at full flight into the westward gloom. It all transpired within a split second, and as little given to athleticism as I am, chances of overtaking the thief were none, even were I able to keep sight of him.

Oddly, given the conditions, I had retained a distinct perception of the man's facial features, and although Astoria strenuously objected that the necklace was worth little and nothing should be done, I insisted we go to the police.

On that particular point, at least, I should have listened to her.

Or rather, I should have listened to her if my goal were to remain in my ignorance and carry on as we had been. I'm not sure whether that sort of bliss would be better than the situation in which I now find myself. I was happier, but happiness is not always for the best.

The closest station was about fifteen blocks away, just off King. Astoria seemed to be in no rush. By the time we arrived, it was past nine.

The sergeant at the desk exuded apathy, and in a bored tone explained that we needed to fill out separate incident reports. Then he went to fetch the detective on duty.

Detective Paul Flattulent was a short, stubby fellow with a self-imposed air of shrewdness. He had thinning blackish hair and blotchy skin, was badly shaven, smelled of tobacco, and wore a loud sport jacket over a striped shirt. To my surprise, he glanced at Astoria and immediately showed recognition. "Good evening, Miss Brownforth. Had a bit of trouble this evening, have we?"

Was she really from Arburo? When Astoria had told me she had never gone back home after returning stateside, I had assumed as a matter of course that she was from elsewhere. Or had the detective somehow crossed paths with her since she moved here?

Astoria looked at me out of the corner of her eye, and flushed with a bit of irritation. "It's nothing really, detective, just a petty jewellery snatch."

"Ah." The officer looked down at the reports. "Deadmarch? Not exactly where I would think you would be frequenting at *any* time of day, much less after dark."

"Just a short walk after dining, detective." She clearly didn't appear at ease with the fact that he knew who she was.

"Mmm." Flattulent shot me a scornful glance, and his tone matched the look. "Not a very safe place to dine a lady, Mr ..." — glancing down again at my report — "Mr Gray. I don't really understand how someone clearly unequipped to offer any sort of protection...."

Astoria interrupted impatiently. "Well, that's my fault, detective. I quite insisted on the walk. I can't bear to sit still after supper."

"I see. I don't suppose either of you could identify this man?"

Astoria shook her head. "It happened so fast, I had no chance to get a look at him."

"I could identify him," I said quietly.

"Very good," said the detective. "Describe him for me."

"Dark hair, pale skin, a rather narrow face but a broad nose, light colored eyes — probably gray, I should say — and medium build. Perhaps six foot one." I paused for a split second, nearly second-guessing myself. "Oh, and he had something above his left eyebrow, perhaps a faint scar or something."

Astoria gave me a look of wonder, jaw dropping. For his part, Flattulent fixed his eyes on me, his own eyebrows raised slightly. "You caught all that, in a second or two?"

"I'm quite observant, sir." Which was entirely true, but still, as so often has been the case lately, I felt a bit off, what with just how vividly the man's features were etched into my memory.

"Well, that's helpful, certainly." He grunted through the reports a few more moments, and continued. "Okay, then, what about his direction? He ran off into the shadows, you say. Could you see which way he was headed?"

"To the west, in the direction of Hafford Manor," I heard myself say.

Now the detective's eyebrows were very nearly up to his receded hairline.

Hafford Manor? Where had that come from? I hadn't consciously heard of the place before. While I had eaten at Diedrich's for years, I knew virtually nothing firsthand about the surrounding area. I'm a walker, but it had never struck me as a suitable neighborhood, either in terms of my well-being or that of providing visual interest.

Flattulent squinted at me and pursed his lips. "Miss Brownforth, I may have some further questions for you momentarily. Please wait in the lobby for a bit. I'm sure Dobbins can get you a coffee or something. I need to spend some time with Mr Gray alone."

Astoria looked a bit apprehensive, but complied. The stubby detective got up, closing the door behind her. He remained standing, his body language verging upon hostile.

"Mr Gray, how long have you known Eric Finsome?"

I was bewildered. "Who?"

"Please don't be coy with me, Mr Gray. I don't know why you're giving up your partner, but it's pretty clear to me that you and Finsome worked out this robbery collaboratively."

Somewhere in the wasteland between fear and anger, my chest tightened and my jaw dropped. "What? Detective, I have no idea what you're on about. I don't know any Eric Finsome, and it's absurd to think I was in on this robbery. I had to practically cajole Ast — er, Miss Brownforth to even make a police report. She didn't want to come in at all."

Flattulent looked like he was about to raise his voice, but midstream he altered his approach. Pulling up a chair backward, he sat down, leaning in to me with that insincere intimacy occasionally affected by bad television cops. "Look, Gordon, I really like you, and I'd love to believe you. But the thing is, see, that your man Finsome has been suspected in these sorts of capers for several months. You know exactly what he looks like, to the level of detail that only someone close to him could know, and you even know where he lives. So please explain all that to me, if you would." He squinted at me expectantly.

I felt dizzy, like a sensation of slipping sideways. Somehow, this cop was seriously trying to implicate me in all of this. Me! Gordon Gray the sedate bore, stranger to adventure, whether good or bad. "Detective, as Miss Brownforth indicated herself, this whole walk was her own idea. I don't frequent that neighborhood at all. The only place I know is Diedrich's Diner, which is several blocks away and right next to my bus stop. And that thief I described to you — I'm certain I've never seen him before tonight."

"Uh huh. And how then can you explain to me that you could tell me, not only that this thief was running westward, but towards Hafford Manor? That's a good seven or eight blocks from where you say this robbery took place."

He had me there. I still had not the slightest idea how Hafford Manor had rolled off my tongue, or even what it was. "Is it? I don't know. Perhaps I made the association subconsciously, from a map, perhaps. I do tend to study maps pretty closely. But I really don't know. I'm not familiar at all with the place. From the name, I'd venture to guess it's probably a block of flats — er, an apartment building — of some sort, but it's not a place I've seen."

The detective shook his head. "I think I'm going to have to charge you, Gordon. You've not given me the slightest reason to believe your story." He scrutinized the reports again, and frowned at the name Astoria had provided, but didn't comment. "Well, Mr Gray, I'll have to get Miss Brownforth to provide an estimate of the value of the necklace, but I'd have to assume it's worth plenty enough for a felony charge." He rose clumsily, nearly knocking the chair onto the floor, and went out.

I sat there in a daze, chest pounding, feeling like I was dreaming, yet all too aware I was not.

Presently I realized I could hear the detective's conversation with Astoria, although they had not returned to the room.

What I heard appalled me, and I winced at the words coming from her mouth. "You fat little bastard!" I could hear Astoria saying. "You know very well that I can have your head, so you had better stop this stupid nonsense right now. I'll take it straight to Drill, and you know —"

"Okay, okay," retorted Flattulent in a most patronizing tone, but I could sense a note of sudden panic in the voice, which I found puzzling. I did know "Drill" must refer to Arburo Police Chief Reginald Drill, but I didn't see how Astoria's threat to go to him could carry much weight.

The detective's desperation, however, suggested otherwise. In an exagger-rated, conciliatory tone, he said, "We'll pretend this necklace is only worth fifty, even though you and I both know you'd never wear anything so *pedestrian,* so if you won't press charges, there's nothing I can do. But I do hope you'll find yourself a more trustworthy companion. This fellow is —" He stopped, and I was certain he was the recipient of a fiercer glare than I'd ever seen from the girl. "Okay, okay, he hasn't been charged or anything. I'll go fetch him for you."

I hadn't noticed that I had stopped breathing, but I felt myself start again. Momentarily, the detective reappeared in the doorway, redfaced. "Well, it's against my better judgment, but it seems Miss Brownforth values the necklace at forty dollars and won't press charges, so you're free to go." His lips went all askew in frustration, and as he handed me my jacket, he leaned into my ear. "I'm keeping my eye on you, Gordon Gray."

Back outside, I looked up and down the street to spy a bus stop. Astoria was quiet, but not that sort of peaceful, intimate quiet that people enjoy together. It was that of someone whose heart is troubled, whose mind is full of something, needing to speak but dreading to start. She avoided my eyes.

Finally: "Well, I guess the cat's out of the bag, anyway."

I looked over at her. "The cat?"

She rolled her eyes. "It's an expression!"

"Oh, I'm aware of *that,* but unfortunately I don't know the significance in this particular context."

She stopped and looked me squarely in the eyes. "Oh, don't be such a buffoon, Gordon! I mean, now you obviously know who I am."

I felt the same puzzled haziness I felt in the detective's office. "I do?" She looked impatient, almost angry.

And then suddenly the gears clicked. "Wait. Brownforth. You're not something to do with Brownforth Industries?" Even as I said the words, I felt dread for the answer.

Brownforth Industries, whose shadow loomed over the city. Thousands of employees, dozens or perhaps hundreds of subsidiaries. An absolute cash cow for one private owner, who had managed unimagined feats of growth without ever needing to sell shares.

"That crazy mind of yours, with that preposterous memory, and you really hadn't made that connection?" Astoria was incredulous. "Well, yes, James Brownforth is my father."

Damn it.

I know now that the look on my face pretty clearly was not what she was expecting.

Because really I am a fool, and I was angry. "I guess that's why you didn't want me to know. Well, I hope you had your fun, but the joke's over."

It all seemed so clear to me now, at last. Why, why, why had I ever thought a wonderful woman as beautiful as Astoria could seriously hop into my life out of the blue and actually be interested in someone like me? What kind of a dope thinks an *Astoria* really would be looking for a *Gordon?*

"What?" she gasped.

"Never mind. I'll make sure you're safely on your bus, although I'm sure you can have a car pick you up anywhere you want."

"What on earth are you saying, Gordon Gray?"

"Look, I have no idea why you have done all this. You rich people get bored, I suppose. But as unlikely as it may seem to you, dull little people like me do have feelings, too, and it's not at all fair to make sport of us just because you can. It's all so hilarious, isn't it, to make me fall in love with you and then walk away laughing, isn't it? Go back to your rich boyfriends and —"

The slap was hard, and observant as I am, I never saw it coming. Which I suppose is symbolic of all of this.

"You stupid fool! Are you so prejudiced against people with money that you can't see what's in front of your eyes? Do I look like I'm laughing?"

She clearly wasn't. In the darkness, I could see the tears she was unsuccessfully fighting back. "If you can't see — my — that I'm — oh, I *hate* you, Gordon Gray!" And with that, she ran off toward a cab down the block, sobbing loudly all the way.

She's right. I am a fool.

Yesterday, I went out to see Mum. I hadn't done so since I met Astoria, and I missed her a great deal.

Plus, truth be told, I felt a bit lonely and empty. Things feel a lot different now. Prior to Astoria, I really wasn't particularly aware of being alone; my life was quiet and satisfactory. I was content with my solitude.

But after these few weeks past, it feels like I am unable to return to what I was. Perhaps it is just early, and I will settle in again. Perhaps. But for the moment, everything feels shaken. It feels like it is not good for me to be alone.

As usual, I took the bus to Midfield, and, as the weather was fine, walked the mile and a half into the country, strolling past fields of sunflowers and singing along to the music of the robins and the Carolina chickadees.

I had called Mum on Friday evening to let her know I was on my way. She sat on her tidy white porch awaiting my arrival, surrounded by her flowers and birdfeeders. She stood up as I started down the short gravel drive.

She kissed me on both cheeks, and then gave me a disappointed look. "Where is your lady friend? I was hoping to meet her."

"I'm afraid it's over, Mum. We had quite a falling out on Thursday."

Her face fell a little, and she took me by the hand and led me to the parlor. "I'm so sorry, Gordon. You must tell me what has happened. But *later*. Let's put aside all sadness just now, yes?"

And so I sat in my old chair, and we settled into the comfortable, customary conversation. "The hens are laying well, Mum?"

"I collected five this morning! That's very fine for the few clucks I have. You know the winter was long, but it all came back good as ever with the spring."

"Sufficient for you and Mrs Shepherd, certainly."

"Oh, yes, certainly, although you do know I love my eggs. I had three for breakfast this morning! Isn't that *terrible?*"

Oh, Mum. I smiled, embracing the soothing rays of her indefatigable warmth. "Not terrible at all, I should say. You always told me eggs were healthy."

It was so good to be home.

Eventually, however, we had to come back to the matter of the "woman problem," as Mum put it. So after a half hour or so of reprising familiar subjects, she took us directly to the point. "Now, Gordon, let's take all of this in hand and weigh it, and see where it was found wanting. Was the lady's character not what you hoped?"

I shifted in the chair and shook my head. "I think that the problem is me, not her, Mum." And so I recounted the whole story as best I could without mentioning all the remarkable details about the impossible effects Astoria has had upon my senses. When I got to the part of the story where I learned that Astoria is really "the Brownforth girl," Mum's eyes opened wide.

"Gordon," she said, "now I know why you said she was beautiful! From photos I've seen, she's a very *lovely* young woman. And I'm sure you are aware — that young lady may well be the wealthiest single woman in the state!"

"Exactly," I nodded.

"Well, well, well. My son courting — or should I say, being courted by — the beautiful Brownforth heiress. Who would ever have thought that up?" For the briefest of moments, Mum almost seemed to have forgotten that the relationship was over. To be honest, I really couldn't blame her. The improbability of the whole courtship, or whatever it may have been, remains a marvel to me, even now.

Were it possible for Mum to be vain, I would swear that this new knowledge had made her vain on my behalf. But vanity is not one of Mum's traits.

Presently, another thought occurred to her. "Now, Gordon, you do realize that James Brownforth was your father's employer?"

"What?"

"Certainly. Regent Corporation purchased H. D. S. Wellworth, which is how we ended up in the States, as you know. Brownforth Industries purchased Regent about three years later."

"Mum, perhaps I knew that when I was a child, but if I did, I had quite forgotten."

"Brownforth has dozens, perhaps hundreds of subsidaries, Gordon. The man himself doesn't get involved with most of them if they are doing well, I suppose. But now that I think of it, your father actually met Mr Brownforth when he received his fifteen year service award."

She glanced at a familiar plaque on the wall, and my eyes followed hers. Sure enough, I could make out the scrawled signature: *J Brownforth*. I had never noticed that before; of course, as is customary, the autograph was nearly illegible.

"But —" Mum scolded herself, "I have interrupted your story. When you found out who she was, something went wrong?"

"I just could not seriously believe that she really and truly would be genuinely interested in somebody like me. I have heard from time to time that the jetsetters and their type can be capricious and do crazy things on a whim. And your level-headed son jumped to conclusions, Mum. I basically came straight out and accused her of just playing around. I really thought that she must have gotten bored and randomly decided to play with somebody's heart for sport.

"Mum, I was actually angry. I must confess that your son was an idiot, a complete and utter dunderhead, even if it's true that I find being married to someone like that to be altogether inconceivable. I really don't want to be rich, Mum."

"But you *do* want to be loved."

I sighed deeply.

"Gordon, you mustn't give up. From what you have told me, and from the amount of time and energy she invested into getting to know you, I think the woman loves you. And if she does, she will let you make it right. You need to call her and smooth things over. It will be alright, you'll see."

"Mum, it's not nearly so simple as that. For one, right to the end, she remained secretive about some things. She just didn't want me to know her, not really. That's how I learned about who she was completely accidentally, after all. I don't even know how to get in touch with her. I don't know her address, her telephone number. I don't even actually know where she works.

"But that probably doesn't even matter, anyway. She was living undercover, basically hiding from her father. Once she was recognized at the police station, I doubt she remained in Arburo at all. She's probably in Chicago, Seattle, or anywhere other than here. Mum, I don't even know her first name, never mind how to —"

"Oh, that's easy, it's —"

"No. Please, Mum, don't tell me. I don't want to know. I've lost her, and I am content — no, I *insist* upon leaving things where they are. For me, she will always be *Astoria,* a mysterious woman with an assumed name, a woman whom I didn't know how to love because I could never know who she really was."

She patted my hand. "But, Gordon, for better or worse, I cannot tell, but you *did* love her. Or rather, you *do* love her. Now that you're here, I can see that, clear as a bell, I can. Your mother is old, but she is not blind."

She stood up. "You stay here, my lad. Let me get us our tea." And she disappeared into the old kitchen, whistling a gay tune as bravely as a mother can. I could hear her pull the teacups down from the cabinet, hear them clink upon the countertop, hear the opening of the tea-box, even hear the flutter of the leaves as they settled into the strainer.

Even from this distance, this power of Astoria travels with me. I cannot escape her, even though she has escaped me.

I looked out the window and gazed at the cows a mile away that I should not have been able to discern. Is this how it is to be, from now on?

Presently, Mum returned with the tea, and we sat together until it was time to finalize lunch. She had prepared a Lancashire hotpot, and I assisted her in putting together an Eve's pudding with custard for later.

I may not look like I eat much, but I never leave Mum's hungry.

After our repast, we retired again to the parlor, accompanied by pudding and tea. Mum had been quiet and thoughtful all through lunch, but now she seemed to have something to say.

She cleared her throat very deliberately.

"We met in the middle of the Depression, your father and I," she began. "As you well know, neither of us were like the Brownforths. We both came from the working class, and things were hard all round for everybody, in those days."

She cleared her throat and looked at her teacup. I could see her going deep into her memory. "But in a way, he was like your Astoria, and I was more like you, Gordon. He was not rich, certainly not in the Brownforth sense, and he didn't particularly aspire to be rich, either — in those days, it was quite enough to survive — but he was someone who knew what he wanted, and was confident and determined.

"Me, I was a shy young girl. I was happy enough, but I didn't put much stock in myself. I never believed myself smart until I saw that *Patrick George Gray* valued what I thought; I never believed myself beautiful until *he* told me I was, and when I could see that he actually meant it. At first, I thought he was sporting with me, that he couldn't be serious. Because Patrick George Gray was the handsomest fellow I knew, and in my mind, he was successful, because he was working. And not just shoveling dirt, either; he was working a *trade,* so for me he was very nearly nobility. Dashingly handsome, and, by my standards, highly prosperous. I didn't think *he* would take any notice of someone like me. But, he did.

"Anyway, we had been courting perhaps three months or so, and suddenly my Mum says to me one day: 'Goodness, Beth, who *are* you?' Because your father had changed me. Loving him, and he loving me, had changed me. I had become ... I know this will sound silly, but I had become powerful, in a way. Your father gave that to me."

She smiled at me. "So you see, Gordon, you are me. Whatever this flaw is that you have, this habit of self-effacement, you get it from me. But make no mistake: you, Gordon Gray, are the son of Patrick George Gray, and there never was a better man than your father. You are a wonderful young man, and any good woman will be blessed by Providence to have you. If this woman loves you — and I daresay she *does* — you have to trust her judgment. She is a lot more right about you than you are. If nothing else, her love will make you that sort of man."

I was taken aback. Mum has never spoken like this.

But she wasn't quite finished.

"Now, I'll say this, Gordon Gray. She accepts you for who *you* are, and you *have* to accept her for who *she* is, even if she has this terrible downside of being *hideously* wealthy."

I knew she was trying to make me smile, so, like a good son, I obeyed.

"And what that means, Gordon," she went on, "is that one thing you *cannot* do, may not do, is allow her to hide in the shadows. You must insist that you want to love *her,* and you can only do that if she allows you to *know* her. I know you, Gordon, and I know you have great capacity to love, but if she really wants that, she needs to let you in. She *will,* but you must *insist* on it, given the circumstances. No more secrets."

Mum stopped and grabbed my hand. "I know you believe this is over, Gordon. Perhaps so. But when you find that it's not, remember what your old mother has told you." She sat there with an air of finality, giving me a steady gaze that said she was done, and that if I were smart, I would listen to her.

Thinking of Dad, I told Mum I wanted to look in the on the old car. We walked together to the garage, hand in hand, and manfully, I pulled open the old, heavy door.

There she sat, just as she has done for nine years. I stopped driving when I moved into the city from Midfield, and Mum never could drive at all, but she refuses to sell it.

"What's this?" I said. "Mum, you've washed the old girl!"

"Well, it's *his,* you know. I'm taking care of it for him."

I shook my head. She had even given it a wax. Even in the shade of the garage, the old baby blue Pontiac glistened.

There, in that garage, I saw my younger years reflected in the shine of the car, saw the day my father proudly brought it home, saw the road to Arburo and back, saw Dad filling it up at the Midfield pumps, saw myself sitting behind the wheel for the first time, forced by life rather than by youthful enthusiasm to become the driver of the family.

I went over to the passenger door one last time, and in my mind's eye, I saw him sitting there, smiling, grateful, happy to be alive. I can't remember that my Father ever complained, not about anything.

We emerged back into the late afternoon sun and I pulled the garage door back down. I kissed Mum on the cheeks and forehead, bid her good-bye, and trudged back to the bus station, feeling pleasantly warm. Mum still believes in this love I thought I had found.

As always, my mother finds the sun and invites me to come out of the shade.

No matter that Mum is surely wrong about the whole situation. She does not know the woman, after all. Astoria is not the type to forgive a wound as deep as I have made, I am quite sure. And I can't track her down to find out.

Still, Mum may have a point about one thing. This woman apparently decided I was worth loving. Perhaps I should trust her judgment.

I looked up from my thoughts and studied the familiar faces of the men coming in and out of the Midfield barber shop, a quarter mile off. I recognized them all, knew their names, even though for them I was just a vague blur down the road.

In my mind's eye, I was again looking at the old plaque:

In honor of 15 years of distinguished service,
H. D. S. Wellworth
Presents this award to
Patrick George Gray
June 9, 1961

Less than three months before he died.

The dayspring on high hath visited us, to give light to them that sit in darkness and in the shadow of death, to guide our feet into the way of peace.

He searches out the abyss and the human heart; He understands their innermost secrets.

FIRST   ENTRY

The two weeks past have been difficult.

My little adventures with Astoria over, I thought my life would return to the dullness of normalcy as a matter of course, eventually. The truth, however, is that I have not recovered. These past few days, I have thought of her every waking hour, and since I have been quite unable to sleep, that has been a lot of hours.

I still do not know what to make of any of it. I have scarcely been the interest of any girl, other than Rhoda from the lunch counter, and even I find her frankly insufferable for more than a couple moments. It seemed — still seems — impossible that someone like Astoria — I have assiduously avoided learning her real first name, even now — could have any sort of genuine interest in someone like me. But over and over, those last sobbing words have replayed in my head.

This morning, I knew that I had to return to the eucharist. I had been absent since meeting Astoria — five weeks. I have never before gone two weeks, much less five, without the familiar surroundings of stained glass, the calm voice of the rector, the cadences of the liturgy, the coughing of the elderly.

I don't think I am ashamed of my religion. At least, so I hope. On that first evening with Astoria, I spoke openly of my disposition toward the predictable rituals, the uncomfortable comforts of Scripture, and the sense of belonging afforded me by the church. And of course, we have said the daily office together.

Yet I had not gone during those Sundays she was with me. I cannot say why, and it makes me a bit afraid.

I walked, as I often do this time of year if the weather is nice. This morning, it was not, but I walked anyway, renouncing my umbrella and choosing instead to pull down my slicker and slip my oxfords into my overshoes. My fedora, I decided, was useless for the purpose and very like to be ruined, so I decided to forgo it.

The rain coursed down, not in sheets, but heavily and steadily; yet I left early and took my time, trying to meditate upon the mysteries rather than the miseries. My head drenched, I arrived at the church steps feeling rather cleansed.

The rector's homily was on that passage where the prophet's bones gave life to a corpse tossed casually into his grave, which seemed to fit nicely with the second reading from the second letter to the Corinthians, the reminder that the present is slight momentary affliction compared to a glory that will be revealed. Life from another, power from outside. I found myself absently musing that Astoria was rather like the prophet, bringing powers and life to me, the corpse-like Englishman, and wondering if that was blasphemous. And then I ate the body and drank the blood of Jesus, and knew that everything good is for the life of the world.

Afterward, as the congregants emerged, so had the sun, and everything glistened with the brilliance of a late midwest morning, a transfiguration befitting the occasion. The rector stood by the door shaking hands, as is his custom. He greeted me warmly and asked kindly if I had been sick. No, I said, just moderately delinquent, but — I assured him — I had been still saying the daily office.

"Ah, Gordon, that is good, that is very good. But you know it is no substitute." The chiding was gentle even if mildly reproachful.

The rector looked about him at the milling congregants, and leaned in closely. "Truthfully," he said, "had you not come today, I would have called you."

"I suspected that to be the case," I admitted.

He leaned even closer, and lowered his voice even further. "What's her name, Gordon?" he asked quietly.

We locked eyes. *How did he know?*

I could tell by the rector's expression that he read my own perfectly well. "I didn't know for certain that this was about a woman, but I do know *you*. And I know that it takes something quite significant to break up your most fundamental routines." He paused a moment, and asked again: "So — do you love her?"

"Honestly, I believe I do, but I have apparently lost her."

"We'll leave that possibility to the side a moment," he said gently. "Gordon, recall what Jesus said. 'He who loves father, mother, wife, child, or even his own life more than me is not worthy of me, and cannot be my disciple.' The gaining of a woman is a good thing — or *can* be. But the cost of a soul is a price far too high."

I nodded somberly.

"But, Gordon," the rector brightened, " you are here, and you have received the absolution. Now go in peace."

"The Lord be with you, reverend," I said.

"And also with you, Gordon."

I slung my raincoat over my shoulder and carried my overshoes, feeling the sun dry my head, and somehow I knew things were going to be alright.

I had not gone far when I recalled Astoria's father. Why were the sensations returning? I had grown accustomed to the heightening of my five senses, but this ... suprahuman awareness, the ability to know things without any information derived from the senses at all — previously, I had only experienced this when I was with her. I looked about me, but did not see the woman.

Even after more than two weeks apart, her power over me still grows.

I knew not why, but I had to see her father. Today.

Notwithstanding my general state of social ignorance, I have always known where James Brownforth lives. He is unquestionably the foremost citizen of the city, and his sprawling house sits exalted above it upon a prominent bluff.

The Brownforth estate is not on a bus route, so I hailed a taxi. The driver had dark thinning hair, smiling eyes, and an eastern European accent. "The big house?" He looked at me quizzically for half a moment, and shrugged. I got in, and here I sit, writing this journal and questioning the purpose of this expedition.

SECOND ENTRY

I still did not know why I was going. I knew Astoria's father was rich and powerful, and aside from working for an accountant, I have no connections to the rich and powerful. I knew that there was something important, that she needed to go see him. But I had been unable to convince her, and we were no longer seeing one another. So why did I feel I should see him myself? What could I even say to him? I sat restlessly in my seat, looking up now and again from my journal and gazing vacantly at the roadside, wondering if I should admit to the driver that I had changed my mind, and needed to find a ship to Tarshish.

I did not. Upon reaching the estate, I solemnly paid my fare, and clambered out. I folded my slicker and set it down by the gate, placing my overshoes on top. I looked up. The gate pillars were imposing, constructed of intricately carved stone. The gates were open, swung inward, a testimonial of chariots and horses and knights in armor.

The drive is lined by stone walls on each side, overshadowed by a corridor of great trees, at their greenest now, in the peak of spring. About twenty yards or so down the drive, a sort of guardhouse is recessed into the wall on the left side, and through a window I could see someone sitting inside.

As I approached, a uniformed man stepped out and motioned me toward himself with a slight scowl and an impatient expression.

He looked me up and down and appeared satisfied that I looked respectable. "What's your business here?" he demanded.

"I am a friend of Miss Brownforth."

"She is not here," he said coldly.

"I know. That is why I am here."

"Ah. Yes, of course. Name, please."

I told him, and he led the way to the great double doors of the manse. Instructing me to wait outside these, he unlocked the door, entered, and locked the door behind him. I looked about me. Immense stone pots filled with shrubs surrounded me. The columns before the door shared the carved stonework with the gate pillars. The doors themselves looked to be solid oak, each of them nearly four feet wide, and carved with the same style of chariots, horses and knights as adorned the gates.

The wait was subeternal, but presently the lock clicked, and the sentry handed me off to a prim little woman of about sixty. "This way, please." Then, with an air of impatience: "We have been waiting for you."

Confused, I followed her through the grand hallway until she stopped at a large door. "Please, make this simple and quick. And don't be loud." She pushed me inside, stepped back, and closed the door.

It was a great room, shadowed at my end because the only light was the sunlight streaming in from the massive windows at the far end of the room. Silhouetted against the window, I made out a figure in a chair. Seeing no one else, I started toward him.

"Mr Gray, is it?" he said. The voice was weak and strained.

"Yes, sir." I was now close enough to make out his features. He wore a burgundy velvet robe over a white dress shirt and gray wool trousers, and looked much older than I had imagined. Astoria had implied she was born when her parents were under thirty, and according to my estimate she herself must still be in her mid-twenties. The white-haired man before me appeared seventy or more, and very frail.

"I have expected you a long time, although rather foolishly I first hoped she would come herself." He cleared his throat. "She shall get most of it, anyway, but I didn't die soon enough. How much does she want?"

"Sir?"

"How bloody much does she want? I don't really care, you know." He coughed, and studied me with an attitude intended to manifest arrogance, but which reeked more of despair.

"Mr Brownforth, I am your daughter's friend. She didn't send me about money."

She didn't send me at *all,* but he needn't know that for the present.

The old man looked at me with a dubious expression. "You're not her lawyer?" He squinted.

"No, I —"

"You look like a lawyer," he said decidedly. "And your name is a lawyer's name."

"I am her friend, that is all," I said, still floundering regarding my purpose in this house.

"Well, no matter," he said. "I'm not likely to be entitled to the truth." He studied me for what seemed like hours, but really it was less than a minute. I stood uncomfortably, unsure of what to do or say. I secretly wished for my fedora, so that I could shuffle it between my hands, or something. Anything.

Then, hesitatingly, he asked: "How is she?"

"She seems well. In good health. And," I lied, "in good spirits." This was becoming a bad habit.

"Well, why shouldn't she be?" he mused to himself. His eyes clouded, and he appeared to be lost within for long moments. "How much did you say she wanted?"

I was a bit exasperated, but I was beginning to understand that his illness was making his mind unclear, so I attempted patience. "I didn't say, sir. She wants nothing."

"Ha! you lawyers are all alike! 'She wants nothing.' Ha!" He put his head down. "She could have at least come seen me one last time, you know. I thought the girl had more courage than that."

What am I really doing here? I wondered again.

"Sir, I agree that she really needs to see you, which indeed is a point I have pressed myself. I just came here to assure you that she is well and you need not worry."

He lifted his arm perhaps three inches and waved his hand feebly but dismissively. "I surely don't *worry*. She's a capable enough young woman, that one." His hand dropped. "But I do know she has plenty of practice in spending money. And it has been at least three months. Wait."

I saw him doing mental math. "No, it's more than that, isn't it? Well, anyway, given her lifestyle, I'm sure she is well past running out. How much did you say she wants?"

"She badly wants your love, sir. I'm sure her job provides for her needs." Astoria had never said that she wanted her father's love, but I knew I spoke the truth.

"Job!" the old man faintly exclaimed. "Carolina Brownforth, working a *job!*"

So her name is Carolina. (Of *course* I was bound to hear her name spoken today, in this house.) My mind wandered to the little bird that frequents my window, and I couldn't help smiling to myself. That's all I've ever attracted, isn't it? One solitary Carolina chickadee.

And then, I nearly laughed when I recalled how Astoria had assured me her real name would be too difficult for me to pronounce. A melancholy laugh, to be sure.

Brownforth attempted a laugh himself, thinking about his spoiled daughter working a *job,* but instead his body wracked with terrible convulsions. Unnerved, I rushed over to him, grabbing him by the hand and shoulder, calling over my own shoulder for help.

I cannot explain that moment, nor what I felt. Something like an electric shock, but not really quite that, seemed to flow between us. At the moment I touched him, the old man stopped convulsing, and his eyes widened and his mouth opened. I let him go.

"Who — who are you?" The voice was suddenly frightened, small.

"I am Gordon Gray...."

"Are you an angel?"

"What?" Now I knew the man was mad. But had his color started to run from yellowish gray to pink? And why was it now graying again, very nearly as quickly?

He stared at me. "Gordon, give me your hand." He extended his, as if for a handshake. Hesitantly, I put out mine, and was shocked by the force with which he grabbed it. In a moment I realized he was trying to stand up, and indeed he did. James Brownforth is in fact quite a big man, wide in the shoulders and well over six feet tall, and his broad face hovered over me.

A terrified shriek came from behind me. The prim little woman had apparently heard my call for help, but she was overwhelmed by the scene before her. "What are you doing with Mr James? Put him back down! He is not strong enough to stand up!"

"Oh, but I am, Miss Edith," he said in a voice much stronger and more certain than I yet had heard. He still looked the part of an unwell man, but nothing like the ghost I had been speaking to since I had arrived.

Miss Edith appeared afraid to come near. "No, your cancer ... it's not possible." She looked about to faint.

The gilded industrialist smiled sideways at me. "I've never really believed in angels, you know," he said.

"But I have."

"Yes, yes. I suppose that would have to be so. Please —" he waved toward the great deck protruding from the room and out over the face of the bluff, "take me outside. It has been so long."

Miss Edith retreated helplessly as I obeyed. James Brownforth placed his right hand on my shoulder and his left upon the top of my wrist, and slowly, we eased our way to the railing. "Don't you worry about my limping shuffle," he said. "Came awful close to getting my leg blown off in the war. Got me sent home early, that did." He directed me to the part of the deck that was enveloped in direct sunlight, and we stood quietly, looking out over the city, sprawling aimlessly in every direction below us, the mighty Wabash cleaving it haphazardly. Toward the north, I imagined I could see Midfield.

Or was it imagination?

Finally, he said: "You're really not a lawyer, are you?"

"No, sir."

He laughed, then sobered. "And I am really not a father, am I?"

I looked at him, and the pause was heavy. At last, I said quietly, "There is still time."

"It wasn't always this way, you know." His eyes softened. "When she was born, we were just out of the war, I was a struggling entrepreneur, twenty-eight years old. We weren't doing well. Her mother was working, too, in order for us to make ends meet, and here was this newborn. I mostly worked out of our kitchen. I'd keep her cradle on the table next to me, or when she got a little bigger, her bassinet was right by my knees. I stroked that head so many times…." He trailed off for long moments, then came back and glanced over at me.

"Do you know, I think she was a special baby. It's like I worked better, thought more clearly, when I was with her. It's like she gave me power to do what I loved. And do you know, I don't believe I was ever sick in those early days." He grinned crookedly. "But of course I know that's all crazy talk. I was young and healthy. But it's true that everything exploded right then, and I never looked back."

"It's not crazy at all," I said softly. "Let's get you back inside." It was hard to hear about Astoria, and I couldn't cry, not here, not now.

I could tell that he was disappointed, but he didn't object, even though I could plainly see that he was the sort of man accustomed to getting his way. We shuffled out of the sunlight, and into the palatial study, where I eased him back into his chair.

"Did she tell you how she got her name?" I shook my head. I loved her, and hadn't even known her name. I had studiously avoided finding out since that momentous night.

"She was our honeymoon baby," he said softly. "We didn't have money, then, my Ilse and I. Didn't travel the world like later. So we just went to the Carolinas, and there she was conceived. So she became our Carolina, the child of our love."

Brownforth still had not released my hand. "You're a nice boy," he said. "Real solid. She's had some fellows — oh, you don't want to hear about that. I know, I know. But that last one, that Blake something or other. Dimes? No, Quarters, it was. Wasn't worth a plug nickel, if you ask me! Crazy man, I thought he was going to kill her, the way he drove. There were stories about how good he was, but not good enough, I suppose — he managed to get himself killed after they broke up, I hear. I only met him once, though — by the time she found him, she already was starting to push me away."

"Good-bye, sir. I will try to convince As— Carolina to come see you." He clutched my hand one more moment, eyes locked upon mine.

"Good-bye, Gordon. Thank you."

I nodded, and started to make my departure. But he couldn't help himself. "Gordon." I turned, and saw pleading in his eyes.

"Sir?"

"I'm too young to die."

"None of us are too young to die, sir."

He winced a little, nodded, and lowered his head. "That is so, Gordon. That is so." He looked up again, sadly. "God doesn't really send angels, does he, Gordon?"

I studied the tapestry beneath my feet and paused. "If he does, sir, I suspect we are unaware of it."

He still sat, eyes upon me, expectantly, compelling me to say more, as if I were a poet, or prophet. I am just Gordon. "We will all die, sir, and we don't know when. The question is not whether we will die, but how we will live. I am not an angel, but I think I can bring you your daughter."

He coughed, a dry harsh cough. All of a sudden his head snapped up, with something like astonishment in his countenance.

"This power you have — where did you get it?"

"What power?" I said innocently.

"What power! You take my hand, and I come alive, and you say, 'What power?'" He beckoned me back and hesitatingly, I obeyed. Still he beckoned, until I leaned forward so far that our foreheads nearly touched. "It's *her*, isn't it?"

My throat tightened; I could scarcely speak. What little I could say could only be the truth. "It's always been, from the day that we met."

"But ... then, she's *here*?"

Brownforth's eyes widened, and he looked past me, as if he expected to see his daughter arising from a hiding place behind the door.

I bowed my head. "No. Yes. I mean, she is here, she is everywhere I go, I cannot escape her. But that is only my heart. I could not bring her."

Clouds of disappointment descended upon his face, but only for a brief moment. Then, it was replaced by a look of confusion. "But if she's not here, how do you — I mean...." He stared at me a second, then tried again. "What I mean to say is, I have only ever felt her power when I was in the room with her or perhaps a few minutes after. I was never the same without her. I always thought that Carolina's magic — if that's what it is — required her presence. But you...."

"Well, at first that's the way it was for me too, but —" and then I stopped, when I realized what I had been about to say.

"But what?" He had grabbed my hand again, and the vigor was returning rapidly.

"I—I don't know," I stammered. "Over time, it seems her power over me has grown greater and lasts longer. I don't know why."

It was untrue.

I did know why. But how do you tell a father that you love his daughter, and he does not?

THIRD ENTRY

As I walked the hallway toward my flat, she was there.

I knew she would be. I had felt her there, already when I was getting into my return cab. There in the taxi, I somehow saw her, waiting, in a simple black dress and a short cream-colored blazer, as somber as I had ever seen her, and I knew that is how I would find her.

She was sitting on the welcome mat outside my door, head down, wearing the black dress and the cream jacket. She looked up cautiously, questioningly, as I approached.

I never run, but I found myself running.

Then she too was standing, reaching for me. "Oh, Waldorf!"

"No," I said gently. I took her hands, closed my eyes, and said what I knew I must say.

"There is no Waldorf, and there is no Astoria. My name is Gordon. Gordon Gray. I am only me. And you are Carolina Brownforth, and everything remarkable about me comes from you. Who you are and who I am is the gift of God, and cannot be returned. Neither you nor I can be anyone else, no matter how much we may please to do so." I paused, just for a second. "Nor do we need to. The woman I love is Carolina Brownforth, and I'd like to believe that the man you love is Gordon Gray. I believe there is something powerful about our love, but its power is only in the realm of reality, not in the fiction of Waldorf and Astoria. And although I couldn't have known it, I believe now that this love is what my whole life has been building toward."

Before I could open my eyes to see her response, she had one hand on each side of my face, and was kissing me. Just as I knew she would.

"Gordon," was all she said. "I love you, Gordon Gray."

And then, I took her to see her father, early enough to get back into the city for Second Vespers.

Pages from the diary

of Carolina Brownforth

Well, Mama, here I am, left down here without you.

I can't believe you're gone. Everybody told me you were going to die, I knew it was going to happen, but I didn't really believe it. I still can't. How could God take you away from me?? I thought He loved me. That's what you always told me.

I tried to say that thing you taught me long ago from your childhood —

What is your only comfort in life and in death? That I am not my own, but belong body and soul to my faithful Savior Jesus Christ....

It sounds so nice, but I don't feel comforted, not now. Mama, please come back! How could you leave me?

Carolina

Dear Mama,

Daddy forgot my birthday again. I knew he would, but it's still so disappointing. He didn't remember last year, either.

Everything is work for him, Mama, ever since you've been gone.

I was brave and called him and told him he forgot. Of course, he apologized. He always does, but nothing ever changes.

He promised to take me out for ice cream tomorrow night, but I have to go with him to some minor company awards night. Utterly boring, even for him. He only goes to these things if he's trying to sell the company. Everything is about business, always. He blathered on about it on the phone, some Bottomley fellow from Texas wants to buy it, blah blah blah.

I almost don't want to go, but I hardly get any time with him, so I guess I will.

I hope heaven is nice, Mama. It's kind of crap down here. Miss you so much.

Men are pigs. Oh, Mama, I wish I hadn't gone.

Everything started off dull. Daddy and I sat with Bottomley — God, I hate him! — and some poor skinny fellow with Parkinson's who they were giving a service award to. He was very sweet. Mr Patrick. Thank God he was there.

It wasn't too horrible until later in the evening. Bottomley kept looking at me like he was hungry, but I ignored him. But then Daddy wandered off and he started getting really fresh with me, telling me how pretty I was and how much he liked my dress, I should be a movie star, etcetera etcetera. Mr Patrick sat there scowling at him, shaking his head, but he seemed helpless.

It was really getting creepy, so I left the table.

Mama, that was worse! Bottomley corners me in the hallway, and he's trying to talk to me and he starts touching my neck and I start feeling really dirty.

And then here comes Mr Patrick. My white knight, even though he can hardly walk. I don't guess he'll be working much longer. He comes up and sees what's going on, and he starts really taking a slice off Bottomley. Bottomley just sneers at him and tells him to mind his own business and go back to the table.

Then right then and there, he reached behind me and slides his hand right down my butt. Oh Mama, I feel so dirty. How could he do that?

But just like that it was all over. You would have never known he had it in him, but Mr Patrick popped him one, good and hard. I still can't believe it. I've never seen anybody's hand move that fast, and Bottomley has his bum on the floor, just sitting there with this absolutely shocked look on his face, and blood is just pouring out of his nose. Sputtering and fuming, and just being all round ridiculous. It was so beautiful.

He starts gasping threats to Mr Patrick. "Why, you! I'm going to sue!"

Mr Patrick, just as cool as anything, pretends utter surprise. "Who, me? I have Parkinsons. Couldn't hurt anybody but myself. But you, I saw you lose your balance and fall on the floor. I think the young lady will verify that. Perhaps you should lose some weight."

Bottomley doesn't know what to do. He's gasping, choking, sputtering, and he's totally helpless down there. I think he's too fat to get up without help.

Mr Patrick just looks at me and asks me if I'm okay and I don't know what to say. So I just ask him, "Did you know he was gonna go down like that?"

And he just says to me, "Young lady, in my condition, I didn't know my hand was going to leave my side, never mind land on his nose. You can thank the good Lord for that one, you can be sure of that!" And he offers me his arm to take me back to the table, but I told him he could take me straight to Philip, that I'd get Philip to take me home. Philip can pick up Daddy later. I was too upset to wait around for ice cream. I told Mr Patrick I could get Philip to take him home, too, but he said, no, his son would be waiting outside for him.

So he gets me to Philip, and Philip and I followed him outside. Just as Philip was about to go get the car, up pulls this car for Mr Patrick. It was Mr Patrick's son, all right. Maybe twenty or maybe a little more. Not as handsome, but I could tell he was just as sweet and kind as his father. He rushed out and opened the door for Mr Patrick, and he helped him in and got him all comfortable, and everything was so gentle and sweet. And then as he's closing the door, he happens to glance over and see me watching him, and he just gives me a pleasant little smile and he gets in the car and he's gone.

Mama, the whole time, I can't help wondering. How come none of the men I know are like that? Everybody's just money, money, money. I'd take kindness and decency over money any day.

Mama, I wish you were here to tell me tonight wasn't my fault. I wish you were here, so you could hold me like you used to. I can't believe they need you in heaven like I need you down here.

Dear Mama,

Daddy is all upset today, flying off the handle at anything and everything. Apparently after I left, he never saw Bottomley again, and when he
called Bottomley's company in Texas, I guess it was made very clear that
there would be no sale.

I never told him what happened, of course. I just can't. At breakfast,
he asked me why I left early, and I told him I felt a bit sick to my stomach,
which isn't altogether untrue. That fat pig had that sort of effect on me.

Daddy hasn't said anything about trying to do something else for my
birthday, but I honestly don't care anymore at this point. Miss Edith felt
sorry for me, and threw me a little party with Karen and Bridget. And of
course Miss Beatrice remembered; she came by with a present on my actual
birthday.

Whatever. I wanted my Daddy, but now I don't.

Mama, here we go again. I thought Garry was semi-normal. Of course, he's a hunk and athletic and his hair is nicer than mine, but you know, nothing too unusual.

After going out with him for three weeks, I find out he has some sort of superhuman strength. I mean, I expected a football player to be strong, but Mama, today I saw him pick up the front of a car. Yes, the *front,* where the engine is.

Very freaky. Human beings are not supposed to be that strong, not normal ones.

Nobody else I know finds men like this. I feel like I'm living in the Twilight Zone. Sometimes I play back that weird music in my head when I see my guys doing inhuman stuff.

What is with me and the men in my life, Mama? Why do they all have to be so remarkable? I know this sounds senseless, but all the constant excitement is really boring.

Maybe I should quit college and move to Oklahoma.

Of course, with my luck, I'd probably find a cowboy who outruns horses.

I suppose everybody in heaven has special powers, huh? Maybe this kind of thing wouldn't seem strange to you anymore?

Give my love to Granddad.

Carolina

Mama,

I just about died today. Or at least, it felt like I was going to.

By now, I've told you all about Blake. He drives like he has superpowers, and it really feels like he *does*.

Today we were on a high altitude Alpine road, and it was icy, and he was going at least 90 miles an hour — maybe a hundred, it was crazy — screaming around the twists and turns. Barely any visibility with the turns, no margin for error with the sheer drop just outside my door. Even though you'd think by now that I'm used to his driving, I was petrified.

And then it happened. We're a thousand feet up, no guardrail, nothing — and one of the wheels comes off and flies down the face of the mountain. The car is going sideways, and I think for sure we're going to flip over the side and plunge to our deaths, eternal and otherwise.

And Blake, cool as a cucumber, maneuvers us to a stop. Gear down, man-handle the steering wheel, brake just so.

And what does he do? He just grins at me and shrugs. Almost as if to say, "There's more where that came from."

Well, not for me. I can't do this anymore. I'm sick of ending up with all these larger-than-life guys with apparently miraculous powers. I don't want adventure. I thought I did for a while, but really I don't.

I told Blake I was done. I'm going back stateside as soon as I can get a flight. I don't what I'll do, but it won't be *this*.

Oh Mama, I wish you here to tell me what to do. My life, everything under this damnable sun, it's all meaningless.

Carolina

Dearest Mama,

So everything is settling into place. I am returning to America, but I'm not going back home. It's never been home without you, and I can't do it any more.

Can't is a strong word, or maybe not strong enough: I *refuse* to do it any-more.

I will go back to Arburo, though. I have to. How else can I come visit you and put flowers on your grave? Besides, Father will never think to look for me under his own nose.

I got in touch with your friend Beatrice — who else do I have to turn to? — and she has been an angel. She's arranging everything so that I can live un-der a different name. She's pretty sure she has found me a job as a secretary — I am *so* glad you made me learn to type properly! — as well as an apartment. She says it's really small, but I won't have much if I'm leaving everything at Father's. I just wish I could go back and grab some mementos to remember you by, but it's impossible.

And my books. I wish I could go back for the books. But Miss Beatrice tells me there's a library not too far away. That will be so odd. Other than college, I don't think I've ever used one. The local will likely be a letdown after Uris....

College. I can't believe Princeton and Yale are finally accepting women now. Missed it by that much, as Maxwell Smart says. I'm not sure I would have chosen one of them over Cornell, at any rate. Ithaca is so pretty.

Oh, Mama, you'll laugh when I tell you the name I've chosen for myself. Yes, I'm going by Astoria. It almost makes me giggle, and it also sort of makes me sad, because you were the only person who ever shared that with me. Ever after staying there when we went to New York (what was I? four? five?), I always had to be Princess Astoria. And you had to have your Jane Austen and call yourself Commoner Harriet. I smile and cry remembering those sweet days.

I honestly feel bad not keeping my pretend name just between us, but I know that if I assume any other name, I'll forget to answer to it, and I'll get found out. So Astoria Pelham it is. (Had to throw in dear old Wodehouse just for the fun of it. Hopefully, it sounds like a real name.)

There's something else maybe a little silly too. Today I remembered Mr Patrick and his son. So sweet, so ordinary, so utterly unremarkable, and yet at the same time so extraordinary.

I suppose Mr Patrick has long gone to heaven too. Maybe you've met him. If you have, say hi to him for me. And thank him.

I wonder where his son is. He must be thirty-ish by now. Probably married and two and a half kids.

Sounds kind of nice.

Dear Mama,

So I dreamt of Mr Patrick's son last night. I guess because I thought of him yesterday, although I have thought of him in passing from time to time over the years, and never ever dreamed of him before.

In my dream, I was drowning, and he rescued me. Which is sort of like what his daddy did for me, now that I think about it.

It's so silly, huh? We've never talked to each other in real life. I don't know his name, he probably doesn't even know I exist. But in my dream, he acted like he knew me my whole life. After he rescued me, he asked me my opinion about nuclear testing. Then, he asked me about what happened that night with Bottomley.

Dreams are so funny. A bunch of disconnected stuff. But maybe that's a portrait of my life, too.

I wonder what it would be like to meet him, now. Would he really be anything like how I remember him and have always imagined him? I wonder if he is still in Arburo.

Did you ever have this kind of silliness in your head before you met Father?

Carolina

February 2, 1970

Dear Mama,

I arrived back from Austria today. Beatrice has been such a big help. She picked me up at the airport and I'm now off the radar for good. The apartment is suitable. It's small, but it's all I want. I start my new job on Thursday.

We know that if we keep in touch personally I'm likely to be found eventually, so we agreed that I would send a postcard every other week, just so Beatrice can be reassured that I'm okay. Of course, she knows where the apartment is, but she'll only come by if she doesn't hear from me.

The postcards of course will come from Astoria Pelham.

Miss you as much as ever.

Carolina

April 27, 1970

Dearest Mama,

I know it's silly, but I finally found him. I still can't believe I did it, but really, I still know nothing. He may be nothing like how I have always imagined him, and for that matter, he's probably married.

I didn't expect to, but I found him. Through my new job, of all things.

Because I'm "the new girl" in the office, I get to do the errands. I don't mind, really. Errands are an ordinary fact of life, and I rather enjoy them. I find their triviality almost comforting.

Anyway, the office had to have some sort of audit, so I was asked to deliver a fat envelope to the accountant. A Mr Clark Green, CPA. His office is only about three blocks away, so that was easy.

So I get to the accountant's, and Mr Green has a big drop box in full view of his desk, so I said "Hi" and indicated who I was with and that I was putting the envelope in the box, and he just nodded and went back to his work.

Well, I was just turning to go, but then I happened to glance at the other desk, and I just about froze in place, because there *he* was.

It's crazy, but I knew him the instant I saw him. That same understated face, those same intelligent brown eyes. And that same gentleness in his demeanor that I saw when I was barely more than a girl. I knew it was Mr Patrick's son.

He didn't see me. But I knew it was him, and after checking his desk nameplate, I think I confirmed it.

Gordon Gray.

I'm almost sure Mr Patrick's last name was Gray.

And so now I feel like a stalker, because on leaving I noted the office hours on the door, and yes, after work, I followed him long enough to see him get on a bus.

I feel very naughty, but tomorrow I will see him. Tonight, I will research the route, so I know where to get on the 43.

I have no idea what I will say to him, but I just *have* to know.

Dearest Mama,

Well, it's definitely him, and so far he's passed every test. He is intelligent, unassuming, gentle, thoughtful.

And I stayed at his apartment last night.

It's okay, Mama, I was in bed by myself. By his choice rather than mine, which by itself maybe tells you I've got the right man, although maybe it says I'm not the right girl. But I try not to think about that now. I *want* to be the right girl. I'm trying to start over, and I think Gordon really is the sort of man for me to start over with.

I have to add that I was also lying there underneath a lovely old photo of Mr Patrick, and Gordon, and his Mama. I remember well enough what Mr Patrick looked like. Of course, in the photo, he is strong and healthy, but it's him.

So yeah, I really *have* got the right man.

Gordon does have an odd sense of humor. This morning, he told me he could smell something called "grits" cooking, and he led me all the way down the hall to one of his farthest neighbors, as if he could smell food cooking way down there. It was like a practical joke, but so simple, so unaffected. He cracks me up.

Carolina

Well, Mama, I guess I'm running with this whole Astoria thing. I started calling Gordon "Waldorf" today. I figured it was fitting, and funny.

He's a good sport about it, which seems to be his way. I think he finds the irony amusing, as he says he's not a traveler, and of course, he's so frugal, too.

You may wonder if I can possibly do this. Your Carolina, the girl who toured all over Europe, getting attached to a quiet homebody who likes to stay in one place. But that remains one of the things that is so compelling to me. All that time, I felt rootless and empty. With Waldorf, I feel safe, I feel like I am home.

There is one odd thing that is happening, or feels like it's happening, at least. When I'm with him, I feel like something is going out of me into him. Is it love? If it is, then I'm sure I've never loved before, certainly not this much, because I don't recall anything like this.

Of course, love is an impossibility at this point, right? We've only started getting to know one another. But I can scarcely believe it's only been three days. It feels like I have known him years, like we formed a bond that night all those years ago when Mr Patrick saved me. Like we met in another life, or are already married in another dimension, or have a spiritual kinship that transcends the normal limitations of time.

Or maybe I just have a good imagination.

Or maybe love is even more mysterious and powerful than I've ever thought.

Keep the angels entertained for me. I'd love to see them someday, too, if I get there.

Carolina

Dear Mama,

What a weekend it's been! I honestly never expected things to "click" so quickly as they seem to have been. I've got to spend a lot of time with Gordon, and he surprises me.

And I'm not just talking about how sweet he is, or even how utterly "normal" he is. He is humble, but it's not that he lacks confidence. He knows who he is and he's comfortable with that. He thinks he's unremarkable, even though he is highly intelligent both intellectually and emotionally. He just doesn't seem to realize why who he is would be attractive and compelling to *me*.

We went to the driving range on Saturday, which was a hoot. Gordon is definitely the least athletic guy I've ever dated. Maybe the least athletic guy I've ever *known,* for that matter. But he doesn't care, and I love him for it. He accepts himself for who he is.

We spent a lot of the weekend reading to each other and playing chess. He is *very* good! I managed to get the better of him once, but he's very detail-oriented and is always aware of everything that's happening everywhere on the board. I doubt if I could have got even one win had he not been distracted.

My favorite part of the whole weekend was tonight, when it was time (past time, actually) for me to go. He pulled out his *Book of Common Prayer,* and we did what he called "the daily office." It was simple and beautiful, and reminded me just how much I missed those prayers and reading times you did with me every day. It made me homesick, but not for the house or even Father.

Strange as it may seem, Gordon reminds me a lot of you, Mama. It's not just that he is what they call "devout," although certainly he is very much like you in that way. But there is something else. There is something calming and healing about him. I feel safe with him, just the way I did when I was with you. And just like I did with Mr Patrick, come to think of it.

Carolina

Dearest Mama,

I'm getting rather confused by Waldorf. For such an ordinary man in most respects, at times I find him — I don't know, *acutely* remarkable.

Do people channel things from other people? I remember Father joking once that he channeled his business acumen from me, but of course that was absurd. Channeling requires that the person being channeled has something to be channeled, and I was just an infant.

Anyway, just how does intuition actually work?

Today, we were just talking and playing chess, just lighthearted stuff — and suddenly, out of the blue, Waldorf tells me I need to call my father.

Why would he say that? We hadn't been talking about Father — actually, I'm sure I haven't mentioned him in days. But all of a sudden, he thinks I need to call.

Which I initially chalked up to a general notion that Waldorf likes the idea of reconciliation, that he doesn't want me to be mired in bitterness. And if so, maybe he has a point. I've seen people who were bitter against one person end up completely poisoning their whole lives. They didn't lose just one relationship; they lost them all.

But no, this turned out to be quite a bit more specific than that. Waldorf told me he felt like there is something *wrong*.

Mama, I don't know what it means. Is he reading me in some way that I'm not aware of? I can't say I've had any conscious worries regarding Father, so I can't imagine that to be where this is coming from. But if he doesn't even know Father, where else would an intuition like that come from?

It almost sounds like something a clairvoyant would say, but Waldorf really does not strike me as that sort of type at all. He has got to be the most down-to-earth, unsuperstitious man that I've ever dated. (Are we dating? I don't even know how to define our relationship. It's so different from all the ones I've had before.)

So that made me wonder whether he's figured out who I am, after all, and knows something that I haven't heard. But absolutely nothing else supports that idea whatsoever. So I don't know what to think.

Anyway, we dropped the subject, and honestly it turned out to be a wonderful day just like the other ones we've shared. For supper, we did go out and have Chinese food, and it was fabulous.

Which sort of makes me feel guilty. Now that I'm living on a wage, I rather feel bad that I've convinced Waldorf to go out for a meal two weekends in a row, especially when I know how frugal he is by nature.

Of course, we don't go to the sort of places that our family used to do. Our fare is very much "working class."

I wish you could have eaten at the Red Bowl. Perhaps you did, back before Father made all his money, and you could eat at simpler places.

Is there Chinese food in heaven? Maybe we'll share some someday, if I get there.

Oh Mama,

What a sweet day I've had! Waldorf and I finally got our picnic, and everything was perfect! Perfect sunshine, perfect breeze, and his dear Livingston Park is perfect too!

All serious talk was forgone today, and we just shared the most natural and fun banter as Waldorf made up quirky, funny little stories that didn't go anywhere, and I couldn't help laughing at all of them.

He even perched me on his knee for a couple of his stories, and tried to smoke his pipe and imitate what he imagined Granddad's voice must have sounded like. It was hilarious! although I'm sure it couldn't have been very comfortable for him, sitting with his legs outstretched on the ground like that with a grown woman on his knee. But he's a good sport, and he knows how to make the best of everything. He somehow knew I'd appreciate it, so he did it. That's just how he is, always.

I came home feeling so refreshed, and so happy, even if I never wanted the day to end.

I know that every day cannot be like today. Can it??

But I could never dream of having even one day like this with any other man I've ever known. They're too vain, or too self-conscious, or *something*. I think Waldorf just takes things as they come and doesn't worry if I think he's weird, or silly, or whatever. He's just comfortable in his own skin, and there's something strong and attractive about that.

And it's really comfortable for *me,* too. Somehow, I feel more relaxed, less uptight, when I'm with him.

Well, except for my secrets. I don't know how to tell him everything. What will he do if he finds out? How will it change how he treats me?

Here I've had a perfect day, and now I'm scaring myself.

No, I can't think about things like that now. I'm too happy. Honestly, Mama, this is the life I want, this simple life with Waldorf and me, just enjoying each other. No complications, no angry father, no stresses about the damned "Brownforth empire," no worrying about impressing Important People, blah blah blah.

Just me, and the man I'm falling in love with.

Can't it always be this way?

Carolina

Dear Mama,

"Be sure your sins will find you out."

It was all going so well, apparently, but how could it last?

I don't know how I thought this was all going to work, getting to know someone, falling in love, and refusing to allow him to know who I was. I should have known that it would have to end badly — deceit and secrecy always do.

And it did.

Now that I think about it, I honestly don't know how it went as long as it did. Gordon is a very observant person, but I suppose he is sheltered just enough that he managed for several weeks to avoid getting exposed to the truth. Maybe in his own way, he was afraid to know.

Everything came out last night when we went to a police station because my necklace got stolen. I tried really hard to convince Gordon that it was nothing, but he was insistent, and I thought that with a bit of luck, given the location and all, maybe nobody would recognize me. I even wrote the police report as Astoria Pelham, but the detective recognized me immediately.

Anyway, when he realized who I was, Gordon was angry, which was not exactly what I expected. But it wasn't some disgust toward the upper class or anything like that; as it turns out, it was because he thought that these past few weeks had just been a rich girl playing around on a whim.

That made *me* angry, because I thought it was obvious how much I'd come to care for him.

I keep wanting to blame Gordon for being so stupid and blind, but after simmering and stewing all night, in the cold light of day I know that's unjust on my part. If I can't tell him the truth about myself, then why *shouldn't* he think that it's all just pretend, after all? What exactly is he *supposed* to think?

When I look back at it now, I know he is somebody who I should have trusted. I do trust him. At least, I think I do ... I just don't know if I trust him to love the *real* me.

Mama, I know I should have told him everything early on, but even now I think it wouldn't have been the same. How does a man like Gordon relate to Miss Carolina Brownforth? I don't even know. Maybe it's not even possible. Maybe this whole thing is a ridiculous impossibility.

But I don't want to believe that. I want to believe that somehow, we could find a way to connect.

I just don't know if he can love me now. Not only because he knows I am Carolina Brownforth, but also because in a way I was lying to him the whole time. Can you really love someone who is lying to you constantly?

Last night, I was angry, but that was very unreasonable.

Now, I am mostly just ashamed. Sad, and ashamed. I don't know how I can face him again. I think I have hurt him very badly.

And now everything is coming apart. I don't know if the detective is aware I'm "undercover," although the name I gave on the police report would be a pretty good clue. Will the department contact Father?

I don't know.

So I've lost Gordon, and I may have lost this ordinary life I've been enjoying these past few months. Everything is a mess.

I've spent the day crying and praying. I don't know what else to do.

Dearest Mama,

I started to say that I have gone through two weeks of darkness, but it's not true.

I have gone through *eleven years* of darkness, and Gordon reminded me what the light is really like. He lives in it, every day, and I have not been.

I think I knew that, from the first day I met him. There was something incongruously powerful about him, as insignificant as he appears to be at first sight, and that power only seemed to grow as I came to know him more, and love him more.

And so, losing him struck home even more. It reminded me of losing you, and then losing everything else that really mattered to me.

This morning, I went back to our unassuming little Presbyterian church in Chase Hill. Almost everything was how I remembered it, but more alive, more dear.

Rev Standup is still there, Mrs Shellingsworth is still there, the Bryan crew, everybody. Looking a lot older, of course, but they're still there.

I'm sure they know all about the life I've led. My sins have been very public. I don't really know how much the Chase Hill folk read the tabloids, but I'm well aware that kind of word gets around.

But I felt welcomed, and when Rev Standup happened to preach on the prodigal son, I felt like everybody was looking at me. Of course, they were not, but it *did* hit home, because I knew that in a lot of ways, it *is* my story.

After the service, I told Rev Standup that I had spent a lot of years angry with God, but that I knew it was time to come home. I told him up front that I didn't know if that would be at Chase Hill — against reason, perhaps, I refuse to rule Gordon out of my life just yet — but it's time for me to come back into the light.

He gave me a hug, and told me he had been praying for just that for eleven years.

Today, I will try to make amends with the only man I have ever truly loved. I hope he can forgive me for not telling him the truth, that he will allow us to start over.

I don't know if you're able to see me, Mama. I don't know what God allows you to know. But I'm coming home.

Dear Mama,

After church at Chase Hill yesterday, I went to Gordon's apartment. He wasn't home, but I waited in the hallway, which is where I wrote yesterday's entry in my diary while I waited.

When Gordon got back, it was like a dream, and yet it was the most real thing I've ever experienced in my whole entire life. The truth is that he pulled me out of my dreams and into the real world, the real world where we belong. He told me that we are not Astoria and Waldorf, that we are Gordon and Carolina, and that he loves me for myself.

It was the best birthday present I could ever have had.

And then he took me to see Father, and on the way, in the back of that taxi, for the first time, he fully became the person that I knew he really was. I think it's because only now, things are coming into the open, and we are no longer ashamed to be who we are.

One of the first things that changed was that he told me that from henceforth we would be going to church.

I know what most people would be thinking (but probably not you, Mama): "He *told* me?" He didn't *ask?*

That is exactly right. He didn't ask. He knew that the only way he could be Gordon Gray is by being the faithful man he has always been, and the only way that I can love Gordon Gray is to love that faithful man he has always been.

He also knew that Carolina Brownforth is a prodigal who has returned home, and next to Gordon Gray in church is where I belong.

So, no, he didn't ask me. He told me, just as he *should* have.

The truth is that in remarkable respects, Gordon knows me better than I know myself.

And the proof of that is what we talked about for the rest of the way to my father's house. Gordon told me things about myself that I probably should have known already, but had been unable or unwilling to see.

"Carolina, I've known for some time now, and you really need to know too."

"What?"

"Despite what you have always insisted, you have never known a remarkable, larger-than-life man."

All those men — Father, Garry, the ambassador's son, Norris, Blake, all the others — flashed through my mind. "What on earth do you mean?"

"I mean that everything that you thought was so remarkable actually came from *you*."

"I don't understand."

"Carolina, I don't understand, either. But I do know this: Your father was never a business genius. He was well-informed, intelligent and competent, but no miracle-worker."

I shrugged.

"Carolina, Blake Quarters is dead — he died in a car accident."

I had indeed heard that — it's not the sort of news that could have escaped my notice — but I hadn't understood how it was possible.

"Carolina, what I'm saying is that Blake may have had really good driving skills, but they weren't superhuman or magical. They were just — exponentially magnified, shall we say, when he was with you. And I am willing to wager you will find that to be the case with every one of these men whom you thought had such incredible powers."

I remember Father's joke about channelling me, and felt like a light was slowly dawning. I waited for Gordon to go on.

"And *me*. You were absolutely right that I was the most unremarkable man you could ever meet. I absolutely was, and I still am. And yet ... I've been afraid to tell you, but ever since I have known you, my modest natural gifts and senses have gone crazy. That very first morning, when I smelled grits cooking — despite what I said, that wasn't a practical joke. I *did* smell them, which should have been absolutely impossible. Just as I did hear the sound of the radio, even though you had it turned way down, and you had the headphones plugged in, and just as I could read the dial all the way across my flat.

"None of that is because *I* am remarkable. It's because *you* are."

I became aware that I was staring at him, my mouth wide open.

"Carolina, there's more. When I first met you, I started getting these ... heightened powers, only when I was with you. From what your father told me, that's the way it has always been. When he was developing brilliant business strategies and decisions, you were in the room. When you were with Blake, his driving was magical. But very quickly after you were not there, they both reverted to their natural skills.

"Like I said, that was the way it was for me, too — at first. But then, a week or so after we started seeing each other, that started to change. Weird things started to happen to me even while we were apart, and the *sorts* of things that have happened have also become increasingly less comprehensible.

"I have a theory that I don't know how to test, but —"

"But every man who has drawn this — this *power* — from me has cared for me to some degree, some more, some less," I interrupted. "But *you* — you *love* me."

He gazed at me for a long moment. Finally, he said softly. "Yes, Carolina. That's exactly what I think. The strength of the effect is dependent upon the strength of the bond, and ... as presumptuous as this surely sounds ... I, Carolina, love you more than any other man you have ever known."

I said simply, "I know you do."

We sat quietly a moment. "Gordon?" I said.

"Yes?"

"I think there's another reason."

"Oh?"

"*I* love *you* more than any other man I have ever known."

He wrapped his arms around me and we held each other in the back of the taxi, and it was the deepest joy I can remember ever sharing with a man. We didn't move until we arrived at the gates of the big house on the bluff.

And then, hand in hand, we walked together into that big house, that ornate mansion that used to be my home, and I watched small miracles happen between Gordon and Father.

I think I'm in love with an angel, even if he is the most ordinary, unremarkable man in the whole wide world.

Today, we will spend my birthday together, and I will tell him everything.

Dearest Mama,

So. I did it. I let it all out.

Gordon went in to the office in the morning, and informed Mr Green that he could only work a couple of hours, because he had promised to share my birthday with me.

And apparently, Mr Green reads the tabloids on occasion and happens to know my birthday. So he informed Gordon, "Your girlfriend has the same birthday as Carolina Brownforth."

"Yes, she certainly does!" And then my dear man finally let the cat out of the bag and told Mr Green about me. I'm sure that was a rather interesting scene!

He told me about it when he arrived at the mansion. "Well, what did Mr Green say?" I smiled.

"Well, at first he looked like he wasn't sure whether to believe me. But he has known me long enough to know that I would never fib or even joke about something like that. So he just stood there quietly a minute, and finally said: 'Say, you're serious, aren't you, old man? That's — well, that's quite a *catch,* isn't it? I won't talk about her money, because that's not appropriate, but Gordon, she's a really *lovely* young woman. I don't know how in the world ... well, anyway, congratulations. And now, don't worry about today at all. Clearly, you need to spend her birthday with her.'"

"Well, that's sweet of him," I said.

"Indeed. So, here I am, and happy birthday." He handed me a splendid bouquet of primrose lilacs and kissed me on the cheek.

"Gordon," I said as I accepted the flowers and placed them in a vase, "I have a confession to make."

"A confession?"

"You remember that day we met on the bus?"

"Certainly. I'll never forget it. How could I?"

"I haven't finished coming clean with you, even now. So here's the whole truth, at last: I didn't just start talking to you at random, Gordon Gray. I actually knew who you were the whole time."

Naturally, he looked puzzled. "Wait.... You did? How?"

And then I told him the whole story, going all the way back to that fateful night in 1961 when Mr Patrick gave Bottomley the business, square in the nose. "When I saw you come to pick up your father that night, Gordon, I didn't know your name, had no clue I would ever see you again. But something in me locked upon you right then and there. I didn't fully realize it before, couldn't quite admit it, but I know it now. Not a year since then has gone by that I have not thought of you at some point. Not constantly, not obsessively, just now and then, remembering how sweet I thought you were."

Just then a thought crossed my mind. "Wait. You don't remember that, do you? I guess it would be funny if you did, but with your memory...."

"Yes, my ability to recall details does occasionally seem rather extreme, so I suppose it wouldn't be surprising. But my father was dying, Carolina. To be honest, even if I did notice you, that is the one time in my life that I have rather blocked out."

"Yeah, I can understand that," I said, smiling at the wistful way he looked, as if he really *wanted* to remember. "Anyway, *I* remembered *you,* although of course there wasn't much to remember!

"When I came back from Europe this past winter, I didn't specifically set out to find you, at least not consciously. Still, I didn't fully admit it to myself, but the fact that you were just maybe still around here was — I now realize — part of the reason why I had to come back to Arburo, even though I was trying to hide from Daddy.

"And then, very much by accident, I *did* find you. I had thought of actually looking for you, to be perfectly honest, but as it turned out, I didn't have to.

The day before we met on the bus, I delivered some documents to Mr Green's, and there you were." (Here his eyebrows raised.) "You didn't see me, but I knew it was you, and I knew then and there that I just had to give destiny a little push. So I followed you to the bus stop and figured out your bus route. Of course, I was a bit lucky with timing, but that part was planned.

"So, Gordon Gray — how does it feel to know that your girlfriend is a stalker?"

"Well," he responded slowly, "This does help me make at least a *little* bit of sense of some things. As I think you're aware, I was never quite satisfied with — the utter *randomness* of our encounter. Your explanation did ring true to me, but it always felt insufficient, like there was a piece missing. I guess there really *was,* after all.

"From my perspective, I don't think any of it makes you a stalker. But it does remind me of another story I heard about a girlhood crush that became the real thing many years later. So I know these things do happen. I just never had any inkling that it would happen to *me.*

"And," he added, "I do think it's rather sweet that what made you think of me really boils down to what I would consider to be matters of character. I suppose it's the only way someone like me *could* get a girl like you."

Gordon smiled, and at that moment of truth, I found him the most handsome man in the world.

He kissed my forehead tenderly. "Now, Carolina," he said, "I know you cannot leave your father for all that long, but I've booked us for a round of golf. Happy birthday."

"Okay," I said, "but for one last time, I'm going to act like the rich girl I am, because on my birthday, I do *not* want to ride in the back of common taxicab."

And so, I rang for Philip, and hand in hand, we headed for the drive-up entrance in front of the house. When the chauffeur pulled up and started to emerge from the car, Gordon opened the door for me and glanced at him, and suddenly, a curiously intent look came over his face. Straightening slightly, and without taking his eyes off Philip, he began subtly moving his hands in a way that indicated his mind was busily re-creating a scene.

And I just knew he was envisioning where we were standing that night in 1961.

Philip stood there, glancing from Gordon to me and back again, scratching the back of his head and wearing a questioning look.

Gordon helped me into the car and sat next to me. He looked straight ahead. "You were wearing a pale yellow dress," he said softly, "and you looked very sad."

I had quite forgotten that dress, but he was right. And I had been so sure I was showing a brave face, but that is just Gordon. He knows when I am sad. I guess he always has.

"I felt like something had happened there that night," he said. "But my father never would say anything about it."

Good old Philip looked at me in the mirror and gave an exaggerated shrug, as if to say: "Who *is* this guy?" Then he grinned and pulled away from the house.

And so, off we went to play golf, Gordon as awkwardly comical as ever with a golf club, and me, rearranging his hips and holding his elbows and shoulders every chance I got. I'm not sure that it improved his form, but I'm pretty sure he enjoyed it quite as much as I did.

Gordon Gray has found a way to make this sad girl very happy.

Love,

Carolina

Dear Mama,

I promised myself I never would, but here I am. I moved back home today. I'm back in my old room, adorned with the same old posters of Tab Hunter and Franky Avalon and cluttered with the same old books by Wodehouse and Austen and Greene and all the others.

But none of that is why I'm here, although I love being surrounded by your paintings again, and sitting at your old piano, and even going out on that big back deck and standing in the sun and looking down upon the city far below. It looks so much prettier and greener from up above, doesn't it? It really must look amazing from where you are.

Anyway, all of that is very nice, but as pleasant as they are, they could never have compelled me to return. I came back because it's plain Father doesn't have much time left. He gets some sort of temporary strength when Gordon touches him, and there's something very moving about watching that.

But that aside, almost every day, Father gets weaker. And this week, deep in my bones, I realized that if he were to pass when I was off working in an office, I would regret it forever.

It's difficult, but we're working through things. I'll tell you more later.

Love,

Carolina

Dearest Mama,

Today, June 21, 1970, Gordon Gray asked me to marry him.

And I said yes!!

We haven't finalized a date yet, but we both want it to be quite soon, probably this fall.

I started calling around to the old gang: Karen, Bridget, Shelly. Most of them think I'm crazy, of course. They're all married themselves to rich, worthless louts, and somehow they think I should sell my soul to do the same thing they did.

But it doesn't matter what they think. I'm so excited!

Carolina

Dearest Mama,

Daddy died in my arms tonight. I suppose he has already said hello.

These past couple months, living here, getting to know Daddy all over again, have been both difficult and liberating.

It took me a while, but finally I told him all the things I had buried inside. He had no clue about Bottomley, of course, and he cried when I told him. He told me he would never have asked me to be an ambassador had he known, but that he shouldn't have anyway. He was so consumed with the business that he didn't let himself see what kind of position he really was putting me in. He asked my forgiveness. I don't think he's ever done that before, and really meant it, not like this.

And it was hard, really hard, Mama. But I forgave him, and I felt cleaner than I have felt in a long, long time.

Daddy asked to see Rev Standup a couple weeks ago, so I called him up and asked him to come by. The minister and Daddy were in that room for a great while, probably two hours, and when he came out, Rev Standup shook my hand and thanked me.

I know that Daddy made his peace, then. He knew the end was coming.

Gordon and I have been going to Holy Trinity. We're to be married there on November 14.

I have become reconciled to who I am, including my wealth, which somehow God gave me through Daddy, which He in turn gave to Daddy through me in some mysterious way. I still don't "get" that whole thing....

Anyway, I have accepted myself for who I am, and all this wealth for what it is. I no longer wish to be somebody else.

But all the same, Gordon and I will not stay here, and I will divest of Brownforth Industries. The degree in business from Cornell meant something at the time, but it's not what I want, and I really don't want the worries of putting it in someone else's hands.

So a couple weeks ago, I told Daddy my plans. I think he was a little disappointed, but he sort of outlined for me the basic course he would take, if it were him, in making Brownforth Industries a publicly traded company. So after everything goes through probate, I will get his lawyers working on that for me.

My initial thought was that Gordon and I maybe could live in his apartment, but I want a houseful of children, so even if such a plan were not otherwise naive, it wouldn't be suitable for long.

And as much as he likes his routines, both of us know it doesn't make much sense for the husband of Carolina Brownforth to be an office manager for Clark Green. (It's already not the same; Mr Green already talks to him very differently than he used to do. It's human nature, I suppose, but it's kind of annoying.)

So after talking to Gordon's Mum, we have decided to move to Midfield.

That was something I really hadn't thought about. But when we went out to see her after we got engaged, and I told her that I was divesting myself of Brownforth Industries, she suggested it herself.

Now, it's probably not what you may expect. I'm sure everyone would be thinking we'd be looking at building a big new house on an open tract of farmland.

As for Mum, she didn't presume, suggested there were surely some nice homes for sale, and of course we could easily build one. But after we had that conversation for a while, it all came out: she didn't think I would want to, but what she would really like is for us to live with her.

Believe it or not, that sounded absolutely perfect to me.

Beatrice thinks I'm insane and that I'll change my mind after a couple weeks, but honestly, I love the idea of my children growing up in the home their daddy grew up in. And they're only going to have one living grandparent, so we want to make that relationship as close as we can.

The question of course came up regarding what Gordon will do. I don't think he would have relished any sort of role in Brownforth Industries even were I to keep it. He didn't seem certain himself, until the decision about Midfield was made. And then, it's like he knew straight off what he wanted.

He'll keep chickens at Mum's. Lots of them. That will give him his routine, which is so important for him.

When I asked him what on earth he would do with all those eggs, he asked simply, "Do you have any idea how many widows there are in Midfield?"

Mama, I have one good man.

For the rest, apparently he has always wanted to write, which I didn't really realize, although it makes total sense, given how the man consumes books, not to mention his silly picnic storytelling!

I told him he could start with a book on chess strategy, or — a biography of *Berry!* — and he just laughed. Then he said maybe he'd write a fantasy novel based on chess pieces as sentient beings.

Maybe I've created a monster!

I think our very ordinary lives will be great fun.

Gordon has already got his driver's license again, which he had let lapse when he moved into the city. It's so charming to see him coming to pick me up in that old blue Pontiac, and then, every time, he puts me in just like he did with Mr Patrick all those years ago. I love these sorts of rituals.

The funeral will be the twelfth, a week from Saturday. I'm sure everyone will expect a big public event, but I will do my best to keep the circus away. Daddy will be buried next to you at Chase Hill cemetery, of course, planted in the great garden of God.

Love,

September 12, 1970

Dearest Mama,

I have now accepted the fact that the life of Mrs Carolina Gray will never be unremarkable or ordinary.

Today, as we stood watching Daddy's casket being lowered into the earth, Gordon leaned over and kissed me on the cheek, and I sensed some sort of power coming out of him into me. Suddenly, I saw colors I had never seen before, felt the breath of the child across from me, smelled the lilacs in Beatrice's hands, 20 yards away, and heard the choirs of heaven intermingling with the song of a distant Carolina chickadee.

I think I may have heard you too.

I cannot see you now, but I will when I get there.

Love,

Carolina

On Wednesday, September 23, 1970, the front page of *The Weekly Gossip* was adorned with the following story:

BROWNFORTH HEIRESS TO WED!

ARBURO — Countless hearts were broken this week, as news has spread that the lovely and fabulously wealthy Carolina Brownforth is to wed the dashing playboy Gordon Gray on November 14.

The adventurous Carolina, already known in her teenaged years as the Grocery Goddess due to rumors she was the model for the Ganton Foods Goddess illustration that adorned cereal boxes everywhere in the Midwest, has been one of the country's most sought-after bachelorettes for some time.

The handsome and mysterious Gordon, highly popular among the jetsetting crowd, is rumored to have made his vast fortune in public transportation and speculative interests in bath products. A trendsetter in fashion, the remarkable Mr Gray has almost singlehandedly revived the fortunes of the fedora among the rich and famous.

The powerful duo's wedding will likely be held at New York's Waldorf Astoria, and attract heads of state and a representative sampling of sundry celebrities.

The couple are expected to honeymoon in the Alps and then the Bahamas for six months prior to returning stateside, where Carolina is poised to govern the Brownforth empire with an iron hand, and Gordon is projected to enter state politics.

www.ingramcontent.com/pod-product-compliance
Lightning Source LLC
Chambersburg PA
CBHW071129130626
46556CB00014B/2995